D1455250

COME BACK TO THE SWAMP

LAURA MORRISON

ISBN Print 978-0-9997423-4-1

Cover design by Najla Qamber

Edited by Melissa Ringsted

Interior design layout by Rebecca Poole

Black Spot Books

DEDICATION

For Stephanie

CHAPTER ONE:

FIGHTING THE GOOD FIGHT

THEY DIDN'T BELONG.

They came from other countries, moved in, and displaced the natives. It was wrong. It was depressing. It was unfair. And, regrettably, there was no beating them. It was one of the sad downsides of globalization.

Fighting them was a losing battle, but that wasn't going to stop Bernice from trying.

Step by step, she trudged onward.

Sweating, parched, and weary, she trudged onward.

Fueled by an idealistic fervor to cleanse the landscape of the encroaching menace, she trudged onward.

Armed with her trusty steel hedge clippers, Bernice sallied forth to do battle with the invasive species threatening to overtake Cleary Swamp. The biodiversity of the swamp would not get shot to hell on her watch. No, sir. As long as she had any say, this wetland would be a haven for swamp rose mallow and shumard oak.

Too bad she didn't have a say in the welfare of Cleary Swamp for much longer; she was soon to get her master's degree and move on to a different university for her PhD. After that, the invasives would be free to commence their bloody (chlorophyll-y) march across the wetland, their roots feeding off the dead bodies of the poor natives lacking the evolutionary defenses to compete. Brutal. Sad. Perhaps inevitable.

But at least, at the end of this, she'd have a nice, shiny degree and a glowing recommendation from a professor who liked her a lot. Silver lining.

From out of her backpack, Bernice grabbed her water bottle—stainless steel. No BPAs for Bernice. She took a swig, glanced at her GPS, reoriented a tad to the left, and slogged through the mushy swamp to her worksite. So many Japanese barberry and autumn olive were going to meet their maker this hot summer afternoon.

She marveled at the unnatural heat. The air was thick with humidity. That was the problem. The humidity. And the complete lack of a breeze. Bernice slapped a mosquito, thought about West Nile and the Zika virus, took another swig of water, and stuck her bottle back in her backpack.

At last, up ahead, she saw a red flag tied around a scraggly little willow—the southern border of Professor Zimmer's research plot. Bernice made her way to the willow and hung her backpack on the usual branch.

Getting her headphones out, she queued up some twangy bluegrass, thought about how Kentucky bluegrass was an invasive species in Michigan, pondered irony, put on her gloves, and got down to business cutting barberry.

Japanese barberry was pretty horrible. It was covered with thorns, which necessitated wearing long sleeves even in the stifling heat. As she chopped away at the bases of the stems, Bernice asked herself why on earth it was that she felt she enjoyed this work. Glorified weeding, and for what? Nothing was going to stop the advance of invasive species. What was the point?

Cynic-Bernice's answer was, "Job security!" It was nice to know that her field was not going to become obsolete.

Idealist-Bernice's answer was, "We owe it to nature!" Humans created the problem, so humans should jolly well try to fix it, even if it wasn't technically all that realistic a goal.

Bernice was throwing some twigs into a pile when she caught movement out of the corner of her eye.

Something big.

She turned to look, but saw nothing other than willows and grasses. Slowly, warily, she turned back to her work.

But then, there it was again. Movement.

She turned, fast.

Again, she saw nothing.

Whatever it was, it had looked big. Her impression had been of a

 2

person, but that might have been her imagination. Being a lady all alone in the middle of nowhere, she tended to freak out about that kind of thing.

Taking off her headphones, she hung them around her neck. If it was a person, she'd hear them. People were rotten at sneaking in swamps. She knew this all too well from undergrad hijinks.

Bernice got back to work, but remained wary, ready to turn at the slightest sign of movement. There had definitely been something there. Person? Bear? Mountain lion? She wasn't sure which she'd least prefer. What kind of person would sneak around a swamp on the outskirts of Detroit? Did anyone non-insane do that kind of thing? Well, anyone besides ecology students and birdwatchers.

She wished her phone had reception. Why did the GPS have reception and the phone didn't? Technology was stupid.

She sighed and commenced her gallant battle, fiercely wielding her noble hedge clippers—named Anduril, Flame of the West. Which made Bernice the King of Middle Earth, and made the invasive species the orcs. Anduril had Lord of the Rings stickers on the handles.

Bernice heard a snapping branch behind her.

She glanced around again for her mystery stalker. She wasn't too concerned about bears and mountain lions since there wasn't any reliable evidence that they even lived in the area. Just a few blurry photographs taken by random locals. And as far as bears were concerned, black bears (the only variety that might be in the metro Detroit area) were really pretty wimpy. If she'd been a raspberry or a fish or a trash can, she'd have been more concerned about bears. Mountain lions, on the other hand, were plenty creepy. She'd heard somewhere that they only attack from behind; she had been advised to wear a hat that had eyes on back of it in order to fool them. But no way was Bernice wearing a stupid hat with fake eyes painted on the back of it. At least, not until reliable evidence indicated mountain lions might actually be in the area. How unutterably lame would it be if she became a mountain lion mauling statistic out there in the middle of the swamp, just because she didn't want to wear a dorky hat?

She was thankful for the stillness in the air. No large mammal was going to sneak up on her unawares. Not with all the twigs and squelchy mud. No way.

Again. Movement.

Bernice whirled.

"Who's there?" she yelled in as huge and threatening a voice as she could manage. If it was a black bear, huge, threatening sounds would scare it away.

If it was a person, they'd probably just laugh, since Bernice was the exact opposite of huge and threatening.

If it was a mountain lion, it'd probably be like, "Whatevs. Save your breath, human. I'm gonna kill you now. Rawr!"

Silence answered her holler. No black bears ran off, no people laughed, no mountain lions mocked and killed her.

Utterly freaked out, Bernice was just considering calling it quits for the day when a hand gripped her wrist and whirled her around.

She let out a hearty scream and swung Anduril at her assailant—a gray-haired woman with matted hair and an alarming grip. The old woman grabbed Andruil, tugged it out of Bernice's hand, and sent it twirling out into the swamp as though she was the queen of her AARP shot put club.

Bernice tugged against the old woman's grip and gaped at her weathered old face. The woman watched her with cold, green eyes, not even seeming to notice how hard Bernice was trying to pull out of her grasp. Then, the old lady pulled her close—just a few inches from her wrinkly, sunburned, mud-crusted face. She rasped into Bernice's face, "Get out."

Bernice swallowed and opened her mouth, but no sound came out. She found herself looking away from her assailant's eyes, and fixating on the plant matter stuck in the lady's hair. Yikes. What a mess. Twigs and leaves and a few yellow flower petals.

The old lady hissed at Bernice, "You understand?"

"Uh ... uh huh—"

"Then get out."

Bernice swallowed again, and managed some words. "Uh ... just so I'm clear, you mean out of this research plot?" She waved at the red flag tied on the willow. There were a lot of random weirdos who thought any scientific research was somehow evil on account of how all scientists are sellouts who alter their results to get payoffs from Big Business and politicians. This lady definitely fit the bill as a random weirdo. Was she a crusader bent on saving Cleary Swamp from the corrupt invasive species researchers in the pocket of Big ... uh, she couldn't even think of a big business that could have a possible stake in this cause. Big Hedge Clipper Manufacturer? Big Native Plant Seed Supplier?

The old lady growled, "Out of the swamp." She gave Bernice a shake. She was crazy strong. Not just strong for an elderly woman. Strong for a person.

Bernice did not like being pushed around. She shoved her fear aside for long enough to say with all the authority of a person who had just finished up a semester in public policy, "This is public land. You do understand the concept of public land, yes? There are laws—"

"That means nothing. Nothing. I swear no allegiance—"

Bernice raised her eyebrows. This lady was intense. "Actually, you'll find your allegiance-swearing doesn't really matter. The rules are still the rules. Who do you think you are that you can order me around?"

"Who am I?" The old lady stared at her with unsettling intensity long enough for things to get super awkward. "I am the swamp."

Bernice blinked. "Huh? The what? You're the ... what?"

The old lady growled, "I. Am. The. Swamp."

"Uh," Bernice said, spotting an opportunity to segue this insanity into the spiel she liked to spew out for random people who asked her what she did for a living, "it's great you feel so connected to Cleary Swamp. I like it a lot, too. That's why I'm here trying to preserve its natural beauty for future—"

The lady let out a hiss reminiscent of a rattlesnake that probably slept curled up in her nasty hair. Then she whispered, "I do not mean I *feel connected* to the swamp. I mean I *am* the swamp. And I want you out. The swamp wants you out." Her grip on Bernice's arm tightened. "Out."

Bernice glared at her and didn't respond.

"You need to leave. I will not have you here cutting. Chopping. Slaughtering. The pain ... it hurts—"

"Come on, they're invasive species! They're throwing off the whole eco-system of this swamp that you love. You should be thanking—"

"I do not love it! I am it! I *am* the swamp!" the old woman screamed in Bernice's face. She gave Bernice another hard shake, then released her and pushed her backward. Bernice felt something tighten around her ankle. She tripped and fell flat on her back.

Oh great. Now she was covered in mud. Fabulous. "What'd you do that for?" Bernice snapped at the old woman as she looked down at her ankle. There was a vine wrapped around it. It might be noted that it was Asiatic bittersweet—yet another invasive species plaguing the swamp.

It might also be noted that the vine was wrapped around her ankle in a way that made absolutely no sense whatsoever. It was coiled around three times. Tight. How on earth had that happened? She reached down and tugged at it. The vine was thick and tough and woody, not pliable like young bittersweet.

"What the ..." Bernice muttered as she tugged. She must have stepped straight down into this weird coil of vine. Her brain struggled to make things make sense. Maybe the vine had grown up around a tree branch like that, and the branch had broken off the tree and gotten pulled out of the coil of vine by a beaver making a dam. Yes. That was it.

Bernice shot the woman a glare, then got to work prying the vine off her ankle. It was so snug. How had her foot slipped into it in the first place? If only she had Anduril, she could cut the vine off. "Got any hedge clippers?" Bernice asked. "I'd use mine, but you threw them across the swamp."

"I? Hedge clippers?" the old woman asked, clearly scandalized at the very notion. "I would just as soon chop off my own arm as I would chop off—"

"Okay, okay. Yeah. Because you're the swamp. I get it." Bernice finally managed to work her ankle free, and got to her feet, shaking off as much mud as she could. "Can I ask you one thing?"

The old lady narrowed her eyes and nodded her head. One slow nod.

"Okay. If you're the swamp, and if you're so mad I'm chopping you up, why are you just now confronting me about it? I've been coming out here for months, and not a peep from you that whole time."

"I've been slumbering," she intoned.

"Ah. Slumbering. Um. So you're nocturnal or something? You sleep through the day usually?"

The woman rolled her eyes. "For *years* I have slumbered."

Wow. Insane. This woman was totally insane. "Mm. Yeah. People don't hibernate."

The woman brushed her matted hair out of her eyes, and crossed her arms. She began to tap her foot. The effect was kinda weird since she was tapping it in mud instead of on a hard surface. *Squelch. Squelch. Squelch. Squelch.* "Go. Now."

"Okay, Okay," Bernice grumbled. "Crazy old broad. Fine. I'm going." Her boss was going to be pretty cranky when she found out Bernice had gotten next to nothing done. She'd have to come out extra early the next day to make up for the lost time. Shoot. She'd been hoping to binge watch some quality space opera television. Oh well. Long after the summer research season had gone, *Space Mantis* would be there for her.

The old lady narrowed her eyes at Bernice and took a few menacing steps toward her.

Bernice held her hands up placatingly. "I'm going!" With that, she turned and hurried away, glancing over her shoulder every other step. At least the old lady wasn't following her. Bernice grabbed her backpack off the willow branch, slung it over her mud-coated shoulder, and skedaddled. She looked back at the old lady again to make sure she wasn't in pursuit.

She was not. She was standing motionless, staring at Bernice with those weird, cold eyes.

Bernice strode away as fast as the mud would let her, then reached into her backpack for her GPS to make sure she was going the right direction.

A loud quack from behind her distracted her from the GPS screen. She turned toward the duck. It was standing on a tussock of grass right by the willow tree. And the old lady was gone.

Great. Bernice had made an enemy of a cyborg with superhuman strength and the ability to transform into a mallard. Weird choice, cyborg. A raven would have been a much cooler transformation choice. Or a swan. But whatever. Bernice wasn't one to judge. All she herself could transform into was an elf for cosplay.

The farther Bernice got from the research plot, the angrier she became. She had just let some old hag scare her away from the work she was supposed to be doing. Why had she been so freaked out, anyway? So what if the ratty old broad was strong? She was just a person. A strong one, yeah, but just a person. If the old woman had been planning on harming her, she'd have done it when she snuck up behind Bernice. Being shaken and pushed around by a crazy stranger all alone in the middle of a swamp was definitely scary, but had she backed down too easily?

Maybe.

Well, Bernice would be back the next day.

With pepper spray.

CHAPTER TWO:

TWIGS, LEAVES, AND YELLOW FLOWER PETALS

BERNICE TRUDGED OUT of the swamp and onto the dirt road where she'd parked her truck. After tossing her backpack through the open passenger side window, she went around to the driver's side door. She was about to open the door and hop in when she saw a pile of twigs and leaves and yellow flower petals on her seat. Just like all the stuff matted in the creepy old lady's gross hair.

Bernice backed away from the truck and looked wildly around. Where was the old lady? She had to be around. Had she beaten Bernice to the truck, then picked the stuff out of her hair and piled it onto the seat? Had she put it there before going into the swamp to scare the crap out of Bernice? That would require a lot more planning and effort than Bernice felt the lady was capable of. But what other answer was there? A bunch of twigs and leaves and flower petals didn't just blow through her open window and settle in a tidy little pile on her seat. Or maybe they could? Maybe the wind had picked up some debris off the road and had blown just right and created one of those little swirls of wind like a tiny little tornado, and it had flown into her truck's window, and it had lost energy and dissipated right in the middle of her seat and … yeah, sure …

Or, the lady had upped the creepy for some reason. Whether she'd somehow beaten Bernice to her truck or she'd left the stuff ahead of time, it was super scary. For a drug-addled, old, homeless, swamp dweller, she was pretty clever and quick. Drugs. Yes. The old woman had to be on some sort of drugs. It would explain the fact that she thought she was the swamp, and the fact that she was super strong. Bernice was fairly sure some drug highs gave people temporarily heightened strength. Yes. She was going with that.

Bernice opened the door, brushed the pile of plant matter off her seat, sat down, shut and locked the doors, and took a few deep breaths. Now that she was in the relative safety of her vehicle, she felt a lot better about things, and more able to think rationally. Everything was fine. With any luck, when Bernice came back the next day the old woman would be slumbering again in whatever den she'd go curl up in once she came down off her root or berry-induced high. It was actually kinda sad, that poor, insane woman living out in the swamp, her mind so utterly separated from reality. Where was her family? What string of events in her life could possibly have led her to these pathetic circumstances? Was Bernice a jerk for having snapped at her and called her crazy? It was, after all, only okay to call a person crazy if they weren't. Was there some organization she could notify about the old lady? A shelter or something?

Yes, she'd look into that once she got home. She'd be being a good person and getting the old woman out of her hair at the same time. Win-win.

Okay. Enough of this. Shaking her head, Bernice placed her hands firmly on the steering wheel. Time to go home. She started up the truck and drove out of the swamp. When she passed the sign that said, *Thank you for visiting Cleary Swamp. Take nothing but memories. Leave nothing but footprints*, she couldn't help but breathe a sigh of relief.

She glanced in her rearview.

Far back, she saw the old lady standing in the road, facing Bernice's retreating truck.

Bernice let out a snort of surprise and nearly drove off the road. She slammed on the brakes, breathed some fuming breaths through her nostrils, peeled her fingers loose from the steering wheel, and looked back in the mirror.

The old lady was a lot closer to the truck. Standing right by the Cleary Swamp sign.

Bernice felt a cold chill.

How had the old woman moved that fast?

Unnerving. Very unnerving.

Well, at least that proved that she could, after all, run very fast. That explained the pile of plant matter on her seat.

What Bernice really wanted to do was jump out of her truck and yell at the old lady, but no. No need to make things worse. She and the old lady had already made mutually horrible first impressions on each other. There was no need to purposely escalate things.

Especially if the old lady's second impression of Bernice was going to involve pepper spray.

So, Bernice looked away from the motionless weirdo standing in the road behind her truck, and tore off toward civilization.

Back at her apartment, Bernice threw her backpack on the floor by the door, made an avocado smoothie, drank it even though her tummy was upset from being scared nearly to death by the old swamp freak, and threw herself onto her couch. The afghan her grandma had crocheted her was draped over the back of the couch; Bernice threw it over herself and sighed. For a while, she stared at the ceiling, taking deep breaths while she recited *The Walrus and the Carpenter* under her breath in a quest to break her mind out of its paranoia spiral. As much as she attempted to rationalize all the weirdness of the day, her brain just refused to accept the explanations it had dreamt up.

After ten minutes or so, Bernice decided her deep breaths and poetry were not working.

What Bernice really wanted to do was heed the sweet siren song of *Space Mantis*, but she knew first she needed to call her boss and give her an update. After that, she could catch up with Captain Joe and his ragtag crew of space rascals. She kicked the afghan off, dragged herself off the couch, and retrieved her phone from her backpack.

While she waited for her boss to pick up, she moseyed over to her desk by her window with a sweeping, panoramic view of the parking lot. She sat down, opened up her laptop, and was just starting to type, "Who to notify about homeless person in need of help in metro Detroit" when her boss picked up.

"Hey, Bernice," she said. "How'd it go today?"

"Hi, Professor. Uh, today went kinda … bad."

"How so?" Professor Zimmer asked in that distracted tone that told Bernice the professor's attention was not really on her. Bernice felt a stab of irritation until she realized she herself was clicking through a list of homeless shelters.

"Uh, when you were out in the swamp, did you ever run across an old lady?"

Professor Zimmer answered, "Sure. There's that birdwatching club and some hikers and—"

"No. Like a crazy old lady. Really crazy. Like living in the swamp crazy."

"Um … no …" Professor Zimmer replied. "How do you know she's crazy, Bernice?"

"Well, gee. Matted hair, disgusting and muddy and ranting about how she's the swamp. Like she *is* the swamp. Like it hurts her when I cut the plants. She scared the crap out of me so I left before I'd done much of anything at all."

Silence. Well, at least she'd gotten the professor's full attention. "An old lady scared you out of the swamp? What, did she have a gun or something?"

Bernice gritted her teeth. "No. She didn't have a gun."

"What made her so scary then? I mean, this is an elderly woman we're talking about, right?"

Bernice should have known Professor Zimmer wouldn't understand. All the professor was thinking about was the limited timeframe they had to work with, and how every day wasted was one less day to make progress and collect data. "She was scary. She just was," Bernice muttered. "And she was really strong and fast."

"Did she threaten you or something? Like should we call the cops?"

"Uh, she pushed me and screamed at me. She … uh," Bernice sighed. If she called the police, what would she even say to them? Not even her professor seemed concerned, and her professor was a woman. If not even a fellow female was going to side with her regarding a threatening encounter in the middle of a swamp, would a tough police guy comprehend why she'd been scared? Doubtful. No one was scared of old ladies. "Look, I'm going back early tomorrow to make up for the lost time. Don't worry. You'll get your data." She felt herself slipping into passive-aggressive mode, and was so annoyed at her professor that she didn't even try to stop herself.

Professor Zimmer sighed. "Bernice. If this is really a concern … if you're really scared to go out into the swamp alone, I can send Kevin out with you."

Bernice gritted her teeth. Kevin was a super annoying fellow master's student who was working for Professor Zimmer. Kevin would think it was hilarious if he found out Bernice was too scared of some random old woman to work alone. "No. No, I'll be fine."

"If you're feeling threatened, Bernice, then—"

"No. I probably just overreacted," Bernice grumbled.

"If you're sure …"

"Sure. Whatever. Sure. I'm sure."

"Okay …" Professor Zimmer said. All right then. "Report in tomorrow when you get back."

"Right. Later." Bernice hung up. Wow, she was mad. What had just happened there? When that conversation had started, she'd been scared and Professor Zimmer had been skeptical, and by the end Bernice had felt obligated to convince Professor Zimmer that she was also skeptical, and that everything was okay. She was such a pushover. Why could she never stick to her guns in situations like that?

She slammed her laptop shut much harder than was probably wise, but it was a just an ancient university computer, so who cared? Bernice got up from her desk and threw herself back on the couch. Grabbing the remote, she switched on the TV. Captain Joe and the crew of the Space Mantis would take her mind off things. Some alien parasite had just infected the brain of their pilot, Zed, and he was flying them into certain doom. Would they find out about his brain parasite in time?

Well, yes, of course they would. But not until they'd had a heap of witty banter and a fight scene or two, and some significant, electric glances between Captain Joe and the pretty cyborg, Infiniti.

CHAPTER THREE:

THE POWER OF THE SWAMP

BERNICE PARKED HER truck on the side of the dirt road and rolled up the windows. This time, the old lady would not be dropping any piles of plant matter onto her seat to freak her out. She got out and patted her pocket for the twentieth time to make sure her canister of pepper spray was there. She grabbed her backpack, locked up the truck, grabbed her backup hedge clippers (named Sting) out of the back, and set out for the research plot.

The old lady was not going to scare her. The old lady was not going to scare her. The old lady was not going to scare her.

No. The old lady was just a lunatic who had screamed at and shaken and pushed Bernice. She was nothing more. Not that Bernice *really* actually thought she was anything more, because there was nothing else for her to be, because there was no conceivable way she was the swamp. The old lady was clearly just a person. Obviously. The fact that she had a body and a voice and the capacity for thought and other such hallmarks of humanness was conclusive evidence. If the old lady had been a … well, a swamp, Bernice would have been heaps more convinced about her claim. Except if the old lady had been a swamp, she wouldn't have been able to make the claim, because swamps don't talk. Because they're not people. Which the old lady was.

Bernice had overreacted to the weirdness of the previous day simply because she had been shocked by that level of confrontation with another person. That was all it was. Bernice was not a fan of confrontations. Especially when they got physical.

Probably the old lady wouldn't even be there. Nope. The poor, crazy creature was probably exhausted after her superhuman strength drug high thingy she'd experienced the previous day. She'd be drained, fatigued, curled up in a hollow log or something, with her head resting upon a pillow of moss, sound asleep. Most likely dreaming of some golden future when plants would no longer be oppressed by humans. A day when plants would no longer feel the cold steel of hedge clipper, pruner, or saw. A new age, when plant and human would be equals, going through this life hand in leaf, in perfect harmony.

Yes. The old woman would be asleep. Slumbering. For another few years or so, with any luck.

Bernice found the research plot and looked around. So far, so good. No signs of anyone but her and a few red-winged blackbirds. Somewhere, Anduril was lying sad and alone, his Lord of the Rings stickers peeling in the damp of the swamp. She really should have lacquered those stickers on. Maybe once Anduril had been thrown by the horrible old lady, he'd gotten embedded in a tussock of grass, where, if Bernice didn't find him, he'd remain for years. Over the years, hikers and birdwatchers would find him and try to pull him out, but to no avail, for Anduril could only be removed from the tussock of grass by the hand of the One True Ecologist. Yes.

All the same, Bernice would keep her eyes peeled for him. He had, after all, been a trusty friend these past few months. They had fought many battles together.

She spotted a Japanese barberry, made a note of it in her notebook, and began to chop. With her first cut, she muttered, "Take that, swamp lady." So she was the swamp, was she? So it hurt her when Bernice chopped off branches, did it? Grinning, she chopped a second branch off.

"Ahhhh!" a ragged scream came from off to Bernice's right, "No! Stop!"

Bernice turned, swallowed, and stared.

Rising up from the ground, where she'd presumably been lying hidden up until Bernice had started cutting the barberry, was the old lady.

Bernice scrambled backward a few paces.

The old lady looked at her with bugged out eyes. Muddy water was dripping from her filthy clothing. She hissed, "I told you to go away." She took a step toward Bernice.

Bernice backed up another step, and swallowed again. Her mouth had gone dry. She parted her lips, with no idea whether her voice would even work, or what she would say in the unlikely event that her vocal cords would cooperate. From her mouth came the response, "But you never said I couldn't come back." Where had that come from? Well, at least it was true. There had been a lot of, "Get out," talk, but no, "And don't come back."

The old lady didn't respond.

Eek. She was so creepy. So crazy. Had she spent the night in the research plot, lying there in the swampy water, waiting for Bernice to return? Waiting so that she could do a pretend scream of pain when Bernice started cutting stuff again? This situation was fast becoming unsustainable. Bernice determined that the first thing she would do when she got home would be to contact as many homeless shelters and social workers as it took to find someone who could collect this lady and bring her somewhere that wasn't where Bernice needed to work.

The old woman cocked an eyebrow, with her eyes still bugged out in rage. "It was implied."

"Ahh," Bernice said. "Implied. That's your problem. You see, I'm a scientist. We science types don't do well with subtext and implications." She backed away a bit more.

The old woman took a few steps forward. "You slaughter in the name of science?"

Bernice rolled her eyes. "I told you, I'm only slaughtering the invasive species. Not the stuff that belongs in the swamp."

The old woman waved her hand with irritation as though Bernice's words were mosquitos. "Once a plant has taken root in the swamp, it is a part of me. For I am—"

"Yup. The swamp. You are the swamp," Bernice said, gaining a bit of confidence since the old lady wasn't swooping up to her with unnatural speed, or grabbing and shaking her with unnatural strength, or screaming in her face with unnatural wackoness.

"Yes. I am the swamp. And now, scientist, I shall speak to you in no uncertain terms. Leave the swamp, and do not come back."

Bernice glowered at the old woman who was still dripping a bit; she must be soaked through, probably playing host to a herd of leeches and other little water critters. "Look, Swamp, I can't leave and not come back. I'm working on my master's degree. I'm doing this research here in Cleary Swamp for my professor, who I need to make a good impression on. I gotta get the data to understand better what's going on. My future's kinda at stake here—not to get too dramatic."

"The … data …" Swamp murmured, glaring at Bernice.

"Yup. I'm telling you, I want the same thing you want. I want the swamp to be healthy and cared for."

"Hmm."

This was cool. The old lady wasn't being overly scary. And she was listening. Time to blather on about how awesome the swamp was. "I love this swamp. I want to protect it. Just like you do, right? It's a great place. Some rare plants and animals live here. It needs to be protected."

"You do want to protect the swamp," Swamp said with a critical squint.

Bernice nodded energetically. Progress. Awesome. "I totally do."

Swamp shook her head. "But your understanding is limited. Very limited. You do not see."

"Hence the desire for more data."

Swamp narrowed her eyes at Bernice. "You insist on returning? To protect the swamp?"

Bernice bit her lip. This sounded positive. Was the old woman showing signs of maybe relenting and not harassing her on future visits? Was she maybe going to be okay with coexisting with Bernice since they both were super into the swamp? Maybe Bernice was emanating more force of will than she had supposed she was. "Uh, yes?"

"You insist on returning …" Swamp mused.

Bernice gave an uncertain nod, feeling as though this conversation was going somewhere, but not sure where that might be.

Swamp tilted her head to one side. "Perhaps, then, the swamp has chosen you. As the swamp chose me. After all, the time for me to find a successor is coming. I am aging. This body will not last forever."

"Uh, yeah. Yup. Your successor." Whatever. Sure, Bernice would tell the old lady she'd take up the mantle of Protector of the Swamp if it meant the old lady would get off her back. Come on, old lady. Be cool. Don't be scary. Go away.

Swamp looked her up and down in silence for a few seconds, then said, "I will consent to allow you back within the borders of the swamp. There will be no retribution. But know this: if you come back, I will show you the power of the swamp. If it has indeed chosen you, you will emerge on the other side with true understanding."

"Uhh ..." Well that sounded weird. "Uh, I'm not going to be eating any berries or roots or whatever it is you take that makes you all weird. I don't do drugs. And even if I did, I'd never take *your* drugs. I did D.A.R.E. in middle school, dude. I was educated to resist drug abuse. So don't even—"

"If you come back again, I will show you the power of the swamp," Swamp reiterated.

Bernice winced. "Uh. Sure. So, let me get this straight. Let's get down to business. Mystical rambling aside, you are saying that you are okay with me coming back to protect the swamp." Maybe she would take Professor Zimmer up on her suggestion of bringing Kevin along after all. This old lady couldn't shove drugs down Bernice's throat if she had a bodyguard. Kevin was by no means huge, but two young people vs. one elderly one was decent odds, even if the elderly one was super strong.

The old lady gave one slow nod.

"Great," Bernice said. "Great. Glad we had this chat. Cool that we could get to this place of ... uh, understanding. You know, after getting off on the wrong foot and all, how we did yesterday."

"Mm."

"Oh-kay ... So, like, is it cool if I get back to work now, then?" Bernice asked, turning back to the barberry she'd been cutting, and gesturing toward it. She turned back to look at Swamp, and gave a startled scream.

The old woman was like two inches from her face, her eyes bugged out again. Really, really bugged out. Like her face might be two inches from

Bernice's face, but her eyes were totally even closer. Swamp growled, "You wish to cut? To chop?" She grabbed Bernice's arm in that old familiar iron grip. Shoot. They had apparently not bonded nearly as much as Bernice had thought they had.

"Oh my … wow … seriously," Bernice gasped. "How do you move like that? That is so creepy."

"Senseless slaughter. Senseless harm," the old woman mumbled, looking at the ground. "Senseless. Their roots are interwoven into the very fiber of my being. We are one. You will leave. You will cut no more." She stopped, and stared into Bernice's eyes.

"Um." Swamp was so close Bernice could smell her disgusting breath. Bernice knew for a fact wintergreen grew in Cleary Swamp. For the love of all things good, why did the old woman not chew some wintergreen every now and then? Oh yeah, probably because wintergreen was interwoven into the very fiber of her being, and was therefore part of Swamp, and so she couldn't chew it or it'd be like she was chewing her own finger off or something. Did the old woman not eat plants, then? Was she a carnivore? Eww. She probably ate birds raw. The birds that had the audacity to eat berries off the trees that were a part of the swamp. What did she do about all the insects chomping away at leaves? Insects were pretty much constantly eating plant matter. Probably within a three-foot radius of Swamp were about one hundred bugs eating away at the fiber of her being. And what about beavers chewing down logs? Bernice felt she'd found a flaw in Swamp's logic, but now was not the time to point it out. Not while that iron grip was on her arm.

"Go now," Swamp said. "Go. Think long and hard about whether you will return. If you do, and if the swamp chooses you, there will be no going back." She gave Bernice a good, hard shake, then released her with a push.

Bernice caught her balance, rubbed her arm, glared at Swamp, and sighed. Was she seriously, for the second day in a row, going to leave without getting any work done? Seriously? Professor Zimmer was going to lose it. If Bernice told her. Which she was most certainly not going to do. She was going to, instead, track down a homeless shelter or social worker who could

19

help her get Swamp out of the swamp so Bernice could get her work back on track and make it so her boss didn't yell at her and maybe not write her a stellar recommendation for whatever PhD program she decided on pursuing down the road. "Okay, I'm going," Bernice grumbled. "I'm going."

She turned and, again, left the swamp, defeated by the crazy old lady.

She hadn't even used her pepper spray. But, then, the confrontation hadn't gotten all that physical. It would have been hard to justify blasting Swamp in the face.

When Bernice got to her truck, she stopped in her tracks and stared. Right in the center of the hood was another pile of twigs, leaves, and yellow flower petals. After a few paralyzed moments, she glanced left and right without any real expectation that she might see Swamp. Then, she brushed the pile off her truck's hood. At least the pile hadn't been inside the shut and locked truck. Now that would have been horrifying.

As she drove out of the swamp, Bernice did not once look in her rearview mirror.

CHAPTER FOUR:

VERY IMPORTANT RESEARCH

"What do you mean, you can't?" Bernice snapped into her phone as she walked into the Sperka Science Building. "There's a homeless old woman—super crazy—out there all alone in the swamp, and you can't do anything to help her out?"

Bernice had made so many calls the previous evening and that morning that she knew the response before the shelter employee had even begun. He said, "Miss, I understand your concern for the woman, but you gotta understand our resources are spread really thin. There are people in need within a few blocks of our building that we can't adequately care for. To go all the way out there to Cleary Swamp ... I don't know ... I just don't think it'll be possible."

"But come on, man. What am I supposed to do? Just throw up my hands and leave the poor dear to die of exposure? She's got no clean water. No shelter. Her food must be just crawling with germs and parasites and stuff." Bernice stomped across the spacious foyer of the science building toward the stairs leading to the basement.

"Look, maybe you could bring her to us?" the guy suggested. "Could you do that?"

As Bernice walked down the echoey cement stairs toward the basement office she shared with two other students, she said, "Seriously? I gotta bring her to you? I'd need a straightjacket or something. A sedative. A—"

"Wait. You're saying this woman doesn't want help?"

Bernice sighed. Great. She saw where this was going. "No."

Silence for a few moments. "Uh. And you're not a family member."

"Nope. Just a concerned citizen. Just looking out for the welfare of a—"

Bernice stopped short. "You know what? Never mind. Thanks for your time. Really. You've been a super help." She hung up, stuffed her phone into her backpack, and stomped down the hall to her office. She swung the door open and looked around. Good. No one else was there. She didn't want anyone to know she was in the office. She really should be in the swamp making up for her oodles of lost time. But first she needed access to the journals on file. Over the years, there had been a fair amount of research done in and around Cleary Swamp for one reason or another. Invasive species, little brown bats, various wildflowers, deer population studies. Somewhere in one of those articles someone might have mentioned a crazy old lady.

She threw herself into her swivel chair, spun around a few times, and then stared at her black computer screen for a bit. That had been the last shelter on her list. Apparently no one was willing to drag swamp lady away from the research plot and stick her in a padded cell.

Bernice switched on her computer. While she waited for it to boot up, she leaned back in her seat and let her eyes travel across the array of posters and pictures taped to the wall over her desk. A poster of native Michigan swamp flowers, a poster of the crew of the Space Mantis posing in front of their trusty ship, a map of Middle Earth, an aerial photo of Cleary Swamp, a picture she'd taken of a pileated woodpecker feeding its baby—she'd won 3rd place in the university nature photography contest the previous year for that photo.

Once the computer was ready for her, she typed in her password and started up her music. It was a 70's funk kind of morning. It was also time to get down to business searching journal articles for mentions of a crazy old woman. Or a crazy young woman. Clearly the old lady hadn't always been old, and some of these articles went back decades.

Sure, Bernice knew this was a complete waste of time. Sure, Bernice knew she was just doing this in order to feel productive while avoiding what she should really be doing. But at least it would be cool if she did, in fact, find any references to the old lady, to be able to show the references to Professor Zimmer so her boss would know Swamp had a history of making trouble.

Some previous researcher had to have run into the old lady. It was beyond obvious she had been in that swamp for ages. Her skin was so leathery. Her hair was so nasty. Skin and hair didn't get like that without years of super rough living, exposed to the elements season after season, year after year, for a crazy long time. So, yes, someone simply had to have crossed paths with the creature. But would they have made mention of it in their articles? That was the problem. Journal articles were supposed to be sterile, professional, and factual. There would be no, "OMG! When I was out in the swamp I totally had the creepiest encounter with some lunatic lady who said she was the swamp! Dude!" Bernice's only hope was in the discussions. The discussions at the end of journal articles were where the researchers would let their hair down and allow a sentence or two of humor or speculation or randomness.

Article after article, no luck.

Nothing. Nothing. Nothing.

Hours passed.

Bernice got more and more guilty about how she was neglecting the swamp for the third day in a row.

She started to get hungry, so she crept out to the vending machine to secure some potato chips. Baked, not fried. One had to draw the line somewhere. Bernice could only pollute her body so much. She slunk back to her office, thankful that she crossed paths with no one on her vending foray. She so, so, so needed to be out of this office and in the swamp.

One more hour. Just one more hour of procrastinating—er, valuable research—and then she'd go.

Bernice was on the verge of giving up when she finally found something in an article from 1972. An article about yellow warblers.

I feel I should note that, toward the end of my research, I had an encounter with a woman. There was an overgrown area I needed to get through. I was cutting vines out of the way when the woman appeared behind me and started yelling, saying I was hurting her. She said she was the swamp. She pushed me and chased me out. She

23

was alarmingly strong, and I was rather concerned, but she never appeared again. It was suggested to me that she might be Rebecca Hallett, the young woman who went missing in the swamp ten years ago. I notified the police. Hopefully they will be able to get to the bottom of it.

Bernice stared at the screen. It was her. It had to be her. Rebecca Hallett. Interesting.

Bernice almost forwarded the article to Professor Zimmer, but that would have tipped her off that Bernice was not in the field. She left it open for later and decided she really had to get back to the swamp. She would have to work sunrise to sunset for the rest of the week to get on schedule again at this point. And that was assuming that Swamp didn't scare her away again.

Grudgingly, Bernice got her phone out to call Kevin. His phone rang and rang. He was probably too busy playing guitar or painting to answer. Heaven forbid he actually keep his phone nearby to take a call that might be important for work. She nearly hung up. But then …

"Hiya, B!" Kevin answered. "What's up?"

Bernice rolled her eyes. "You busy?"

"Nah. Just down by the water playing guitar. Why?"

Playing guitar. She had called it. Kevin was such a slacker. How he got decent grades was beyond Bernice. His days were so full of painting and writing songs and playing in his folk band in the evenings that Bernice had no idea how he managed to fit studying in. But on top of all his arty crap, he was also a great student. Bernice kinda hated him. "I need you to come out to Cleary Swamp with me. Cool?"

"Sure thing. You okay?"

"Yeah. I'm fine. Why?"

"Professor Zimmer mentioned—"

Bernice did not want to hear Professor Zimmer's misinterpreted slant on Bernice's paranoia. And more, she didn't want to hear Professor Zimmer's misinterpreted slant filtered through Kevin's misinterpretation. She cut him off before he could start. "I'm at the science building. My truck's in the back lot. Meet me there as soon as you can."

"Wait, wait, wait," said Kevin. "We're going to what?"

Bernice sighed and glanced at her shaggy-haired, bearded companion. "Going to bring a crazy old lady to a homeless shelter," she said slowly, as though she was talking to a child. Or an idiot (which, in her opinion, she was). Honestly. She'd explained it once already. Did he need her to put together a PowerPoint presentation? Did he need a lecture with handouts and the threat of an exam hanging over his head? Or maybe he could only understand things written out in the form of stupid wannabe Bob Dylan lyrics.

Kevin went on, "And this homeless woman lives in Cleary Swamp?"

"Yep."

"And she doesn't want to leave?"

"I don't know that yet."

"Well, I mean, she's gotta want to be there, right? Like she's not lost. Yeah? Sounds like she's been living there for ages."

"Yeah, if her hair is any indication."

"Well then, B, she must wanna be there if she's been there a long time," Kevin said, speaking slow as though he was talking to a child. Or an idiot.

Bernice glared. "Not necessarily."

"But … uh … yeah. Like, the swamp's big, but it's nothing a person couldn't trek across in two days and spot some sort of civilization. If she wanted to leave, she could have done so any time just by putting one foot in front of the other and finding a house in a day or three."

Bernice frowned. "Sure. But if she's crazy I don't think logic really applies, Kevin."

"Maybe. But with all the research and hiking and stuff that goes on in the swamp, I fail to see how she wouldn't have been found ages ago unless she didn't want to be. Like maybe she's just a hobo who chooses that lifestyle."

Bernice rolled her eyes. "No one would choose that life."

"I dunno, B, maybe you're just saying that because of your frame of reference. It's hard to understand poverty or alternate ways of living if you've lived an easy life."

Bernice scoffed, "Oh, and you're so enlightened and world-wise, Mr. Private School Grosse Point rich boy?" She turned off onto the dirt road that ran into the swamp.

"Wow, B. Chill out. No need to get personal."

Bernice growled, "I hate when people tell me to calm down. Does that ever work? Like do you ever tell someone to chill out and they actually do it?"

Kevin cleared his throat. "Sorry."

Bernice looked away from the road to glare at him. She snapped, "I didn't ask you along so you could irritate me and argue and tell me to chill out. I asked you along for help."

"Eyes on the road, B," Kevin said, pointing ahead of them.

Bernice stupidly gave him a bit more of a glare just to see the nervousness in his eyes as she drove without looking. Then she turned back to the road. "Got me? I don't wanna argue about whether she's crazy or whether she wants to leave. Let's just go and find out."

"Sure, sure. Fine," he muttered, folding his arms and slouching away from her.

They drove on in silence for a bit. Bernice was aware Kevin kept glancing at her, but she ignored him.

After a bit, he said, "Sorry, B. Didn't mean to make you mad. I just wanna understand the situation I'm getting into."

Bernice clenched her teeth and was quiet for a few seconds, then muttered, "I guess you've got a right to ask questions. You okay with the plan?"

"Uh, I guess so? I dunno. I mean, if she doesn't want to come we're not going to force her, right? We're not going to grab her and drag her out of the swamp against her will, are we?"

"No," Bernice said, though if it weren't for the old lady's superhuman strength, Bernice had to admit she might have been tempted to drag her to the homeless shelter against her will. "No, we won't force her. But I just gotta see if I can talk her into it. Okay?"

"Sure. Sure." He gave her a sidelong glance.

"What, Kevin?" she hissed as she parked the truck in her usual spot.

"You're really on edge."

"Uh, yeah I'm on edge. I just explained the past two days to you. It should be clear why I'm on edge." She got out of the truck, slammed the door, grabbed her backup clippers out of the back, and tromped into the swamp without a backward glance.

CHAPTER FIVE:

ASIATIC BITTERSWEET

BEHIND BERNICE, THE passenger door slammed and Kevin called, "Wait up!"

She slowed a bit.

"You still mad at me?" he asked from behind her as he crashed through the underbrush, probably snapping branches and sending stabs of pain through the fiber of Swamp's being. Not that Bernice really thought that. But it did enter her mind. In a totally not believing kind of way. Totally not believing.

"No. I'm not mad. This is all just so frustrating."

"Totally. Totally," Kevin said as he caught up and fell into step beside her. "Look, I'm not doubting you here. I'm sure this lady's every bit as creepy as you say she is. I'm just saying you're totally on edge and maybe you should take a pause. Take some breaths. Get some perspective. If you're gonna be trying to talk her into leaving her home and going somewhere she probably doesn't want to go, you better be in a good place mentally. Yeah? She's gonna catch your stress vibes and she's gonna be all on edge, too. Yeah?"

Bernice gritted her teeth and adjusted her backpack on her shoulder. "Did I for ask your advice?"

"No. But you did ask for my help."

"That doesn't mean you get to—" she started, then stopped herself. Why was she being mean to him? Poor Kevin. It wasn't his fault he bugged her so much. So what if he floated through life without a care in the world and everything always magically fell into place for him? He'd never done a thing to her other than help her out when she asked him to. "Sorry, man. Sorry."

He shrugged. "Don't worry about it. You've got stuff going on."

They trudged on.

Kevin persisted, "So, if she doesn't want to come to the shelter?"

"Uh, well I guess then we … uh …"

He snorted, "Nice plan, B. Really." He shot her a grin. "Hopefully once you've got a master's under your belt you'll be able to throw together a plan of attack a bit easier."

She laughed. "Yeah, who knows."

"So we just wing it?"

"Yeah. Just wing it."

"And wing it will probably mean turn tail and run when the old lady starts talking crazy?"

Bernice smiled. "Quite likely."

They walked through a little thicket of alders. Bernice went first. One of the branches she pushed out of the way flew back and smacked Kevin in the face.

"Ouch! Watch it!" he gasped.

She whirled. "Oh! Sorry, Kevin—"

"No worries," he said, though he looked irritated. He grabbed the skinny little branch and snapped it from the trunk.

Bernice gasped. The old woman would feel it. But—

Bernice got ahold of herself. The old woman had *not* felt the branch break. She was not the swamp. That was not within the realm of possibility. Bernice forced herself to turn and walk away.

She heard Kevin start up again, too. Then he gave a gasp.

Bernice ignored him and walked on. He'd probably just slipped in the mud.

Kevin uttered a cry of pain, and there was the sound of something heavy hitting the ground. He swore and yelled, "Bernice!"

Bernice rolled her eyes. The klutz. That's what he got for not wearing his hiking boots. Not that he'd had a chance to go home and get them, because she'd made it clear she needed him to meet her at her truck ASAP. Whatever. She turned. "Come on, Kevin. Get up."

He was on the ground, lying in the mud among the roots of an alder, clutching his ankle. "Ouch. Wow. Ow," he gasped.

Bernice backtracked and knelt in the mud beside him. "What's wrong with it?" she sighed. This trip was not going well. "Twisted?"

He took in a ragged breath. "This really hurts. I think ... shoot, B, I think it's broken."

Bernice looked at his ankle and valiantly refrained from grumbling under her breath about the inconvenience. She did *not* want to drag Kevin out of the swamp or have to function as a human crutch. They were pretty far in.

As he writhed in the mud, she sat back on her heels and thought a few seconds.

Then she looked back at his ankle.

She squinted. "What's that?"

Under his hands, she could see a vine. A thick Asiatic bittersweet.

Uh oh.

She swallowed, thinking of the vine that had gotten wrapped around her ankle the previous day. She put her hands on his wrists, and pulled his hands away. Oh no. The vine was coiled tightly around his ankle four times. She met Kevin's gaze.

He looked wildly from her to the vine and back again. "How ... how did that ... happen?"

"We gotta get you out of here," she said, looking around. Please, old lady, stay away. Please.

"Bernice ... this vine is— How?" he asked, panicked.

"You must have stepped down into it just right?" She positioned the hedge clippers to cut him free. *The old lady would not feel it. She would not. She was just a person. She wasn't anything supernatural. That was insane. This was reality.*

Kevin rambled, "This is weird. It doesn't make sense—" He stopped short and looked past Bernice.

She didn't have to turn to know why he suddenly seemed terrified. The old woman was behind her. Bernice froze. She did not want to turn. Maybe it was not the old woman. Maybe it was a bear or a mountain lion. Please. Bernice met Kevin's wide eyes. "It's her, isn't it?"

He gave a slow nod.

Bernice still didn't turn. Gritting her teeth, she started to cut the vine, and was just about to slice through it when a powerful blow to her back sent her flying over Kevin. She hit the ground a few feet away from him, gasping and winded. She turned her head and saw the old woman striding over to Kevin, standing over him, looking down at him with a detached sort of interest.

"Who is this?" Swamp asked Bernice.

"I'm Kevin ..." he whispered, his gaze bouncing from her to Bernice with shock. "You Okay, B?"

Bernice took a moment to assess her body. Wow. That had just happened. The old woman had actually just hit her with enough force to launch her through the air. Not cool. Her back hurt. "I'm okay," she muttered.

Swamp growled at Bernice, "Who is this ... Kevin?"

"He's a friend," Bernice replied, though 'friend' was stretching it. "We came to talk to you about—"

"He cannot know the secret of the swamp."

Bernice sighed. "This is nothing to do with that. I didn't come back for that."

"I told you if you came back I'd show you the secret of the swamp."

"Uh, sure you did, but that doesn't mean I'm interested," Bernice sighed. "I just wanted to tell you about this place downtown where you can go and—"

"You should not have brought him," Swamp said, glaring down at Kevin.

Bernice saw something creepy in the old woman's eyes as she looked at Kevin. Wincing with pain, Bernice started to get to her feet. "Hey, what's up? What are you—"

The old woman snapped, "He shouldn't be here. He can't see what comes next. I'll have to—"

Kevin looked wildly from the old woman to Bernice and back again. "Hey ... hold on," he said. "Let's just talk—"

31

The old woman reached into the folds of her filthy clothing. Her hand emerged, fist clenched around something, and she hunkered down by him.

He tried to back away, but his ankle was caught tight. "Hey now ... whatever's going on here, it doesn't have to go like—"

The old lady cut him off, peering over her shoulder at Bernice, who was walking cautiously over to her as though approaching a rabid beast. "You were not supposed to bring a companion," the old woman hissed at Bernice.

"You never told me that!" Bernice said. "You really need to be more clear about your rules, lady." She crept closer, trying to figure out what she could even do if she got close enough to help. The old lady would just send her flying again. Bernice swallowed nervously as Swamp turned back to Kevin and brought her fist slowly toward his face. Swamp gave him an ominous sort of grin.

His eyes widened and he struggled against the vine. "Bernice?" he asked as he stared at the old lady's hand, which was moving closer and closer to his face.

Kevin gave Swamp's hand a convulsive slap.

Swamp growled, and snapped her fingers.

Right after the snap, there was a rustling sound from the trunk of one of the nearby alders. Swamp looked expectantly toward the sound.

Bernice followed her gaze. The sound was coming from one of the trees. A bird, maybe? A squirrel? What?

Oh.

Bernice saw it and stopped in her tracks, staring. Her brain could not accept it. It made no sense.

A vine of Asiatic bittersweet was uncoiling itself from one of the alders. Bernice's mouth went dry. That vine had moved. That vine had just actually moved. And not only had it moved, but it was still moving. It was uncoiling like a snake. Bernice blinked and shook her head and could not believe what she was seeing.

"Bernice ..." Kevin moaned. "Bernice, what the—"

Tearing her gaze from the vine that was now sliding its way toward

Kevin, she roared at the old lady, "Get away from him! Stop it! He's got nothing to do with this!" She started to move again, having no idea what to do, but knowing that if something happened to Kevin it would be all her fault.

"You should not have brought him," the old lady repeated. Bernice reached Swamp and grabbed at her. Why? She had no idea. Not the slightest idea what she hoped to accomplish.

The old lady hit her and sent her flying through the air again.

Bernice hit the ground and skidded through the mud, sliding to a halt at the base of another alder. She blinked, and winced at the pain in her shoulder. She looked at Kevin. He was staring, terrified, struggling, as the vine wrapped itself around his left wrist. Then, his right wrist.

"Stop it!" Bernice screamed. "Leave him alone!"

Ignoring Bernice, the old lady hunkered down again by Kevin, opened her fist, palm upward, and blew on her hand. Some powder flew into Kevin's face.

He coughed and met Bernice's gaze. He looked so scared. Beyond scared.

The old woman stood and backed away a few paces, brushing her hands off on her filthy clothing.

Bernice pushed herself to her feet again and flew to Kevin's side. "Are you okay?" she gasped, looking into his eyes.

"I … uh, I think so? What'd she do?"

They both looked up at the old woman.

She smirked down at them.

Bernice screeched, "What did you do? What was that stuff?"

The old woman didn't respond.

"Bernice …" Kevin said. "Uh … Bernice something's … wrong …"

Bernice turned back to him. His head was swaying left and right. His eyes were unfocused. She put her hands on either side of his head. "Kevin!"

He stared at the air over her left shoulder and giggled.

"Kevin! Can you hear me?" she yelled. She looked at the old woman. "What did you do to him?"

Kevin kept on giggling. His lips were blue.

"Is he—" Bernice gasped, peering down at him. "Is he going to—" She couldn't finish the question. "Oh no. No." She looked up again at the old woman. In the space of time it had taken Bernice to glance down at Kevin and up again, the old woman had moved silently to stand right behind her.

"Come," the old woman said, leaning down and grabbing Bernice by the elbow. She effortlessly pulled Bernice to her feet.

"No! I need to get him to the hospital!"

The old woman just pulled her, without saying a word.

Bernice tried to shake her off. "He's going to die! Let me take him to the hospital!" She looked down at Kevin again. He had rested his head in the mud and was staring up at the sky, still giggling. "Just let me take him to the hospital! I swear, I'll come right back here after—"

"Come along," the old woman instructed as she continued to pull. Bernice grabbed a tree, but the old woman yanked her free and dragged her on a few more paces.

Bernice's eyes were still glued on Kevin. He didn't have his backpack. He must have left it in the truck. That meant he didn't have water. He might not have his phone, either. Not that there was reception in the swamp. Could he make it back to the truck on that ankle once he woke? Because wake up he would. He was not going to die. The old lady had to be telling the truth. She had to have been. Kevin could not die.

After a moment of hesitation, Bernice took her backpack off her shoulder and tossed it at Kevin. It squelched into the mud at his side. Now he had water and a phone.

After a moment, she tossed her hedge clippers toward him, too. With his hands caught by the vine, would he even be able to get himself free once that powder stuff had gotten out of his system? If it did? "You sure he'll live?" she gasped as she was pulled deeper into the swamp.

"Yes."

"Are you just saying that to shut me up?" Bernice tripped over a root.

"No. It is true. I do not kill. Not even humans."

"You talk like you're not one," Bernice said, trying to twist out of Swamp's grip. "You. Are. Not. The. Swamp."

Swamp just answered calmly, "You will understand soon enough."

One more tug and Bernice could no longer see Kevin. A few seconds later, his creepy giggling stopped abruptly. Oh no. Sure, he was annoying, but still Bernice didn't want to have led the guy to his death. Death all alone in the middle of the swamp. Death by weird poison powder. At least if he was dead it looked like his death had been … uh … enjoyable? The way he'd been laughing, it at least probably hadn't been painful.

She swallowed heavily and directed her attention to the old woman. Time to struggle some more. She dug her heels into the mud, but the old lady simply pulled her along. Bernice's boots made two long grooves in the muck until she hit another root and tripped.

The old lady didn't stop to give her time to right herself. Bernice fell to one knee. Before Bernice had a chance to get to her feet, she was pulled from her knees and found herself being dragged along on her stomach. Over roots, through grasses and mud. She felt some jagged something catch on her cheek and slice her skin. A ground-level branch caught and stuck in her hair; Bernice cried out in pain as Swamp tugged her away from the tree and the branch pulled out some of her hair. "Stop!" Bernice gasped, getting a mouthful of mud.

The old woman didn't answer.

"You can't do this!" Bernice gasped, in the face of all evidence to the contrary.

Still no answer.

Somehow, Bernice managed to twist and do a little jumping maneuver, wrenching herself to her feet. She panted, "Where are we going?"

"To the heart of the swamp."

CHAPTER SIX:

A SUCCESSOR

THEY HAD BEEN slogging through the swamp for a half hour. Bernice had screamed and struggled at first, but there's only so much struggling one can do when being pulled through a swamp by a crazy, single-minded, super-strong old lady swamp cyborg, or whatever she was. Swamp just led Bernice along behind her, not appearing to tire at all.

So, Bernice gave up.

Exactly what a kidnapping victim should never do.

She was a disgrace to the personal defense class she'd taken as a fresh-man. That nice, shiny A had looked so good on her report card, and she'd felt pretty sure she'd learned enough to manage all right if she ever found herself in a situation where she needed to defend herself. But apparently practic-ing defending oneself against a pretend assailant on an exercise mat in the Student Development Complex was not, after all, the same as the real thing. Especially when the real thing involved a swamp cyborg witch.

Instead of struggling and screaming, she decided to ask questions in-stead. "And you're certain my friend will be okay? I mean," she swatted a mosquito out of her face, "his lips were blue. Pretty sure that means he's not getting enough air—"

"He will awaken with the sunrise."

"Wait, he'll be unconscious all night?" That was less than ideal. Better than dead, sure. But worse than it might be. Poor Kevin. Bernice hoped her phone was charged enough to make it through the night. She hoped he found it in her backpack.

The old woman didn't answer Bernice's question, perhaps because tech-nically she already had.

Bernice decided that, though she was still far from reassured about Kevin, she was about as reassured as she was likely to get. So, she changed topics. "You can't just drag me off into the swamp."

"But that is precisely what I am doing, and, as you see, it appears to be working."

She had a point.

Bernice glared at the old woman, and continued, "People will notice I'm gone. And the first place they'll search is the swamp. Because they'll know that's where I am, because that's where I always am." And, of course, Kevin knew she was here and would tell people tomorrow once he had woken up and found his way back to civilization somehow. But she was not going to draw the old lady's attention to that. Not while Kevin was unconscious and injured and unable to defend himself. Bernice didn't have much faith in Swamp's pronouncement that she wouldn't kill. If it meant covering her tracks, Bernice could easily imagine this evil old lady killing Kevin.

"They will not find you if the swamp does not want you to be found."

Bernice swallowed heavily. If this old lady really was the Rebecca Hallett who had disappeared in the swamp in the 1960s and had never been found, she clearly knew a thing or two about evading people. Bernice had a depressing amount of faith in the woman's ability to keep her from being found by the people who would hopefully be searching for her.

"So how long am I going to be here?" Bernice asked. "Like you're going to show me the secret of the swamp and then what? Then I go?"

"The swamp will decide."

"But I thought you were the swamp." Bernice felt the cut on her face. Her cheek was bleeding pretty bad.

"I am the swamp," Swamp agreed.

"Then doesn't that mean you'll decide?"

"No."

"But if the swamp will decide, and you are the swamp, it logically follows—"

"I am not the entirety of the swamp. The swamp covers a vast area of land. I do not."

"Sure. I get that," Bernice panted, growing weary of the pace the old lady was setting. "But you certainly seem to think you're the consciousness of the swamp. Or like its ambassador or whatever. Yes?"

"Yes. Its ambassador."

"Then … if you know the mind of the swamp, you know what the swamp will decide about me." It was so hard reasoning with crazy. Especially when crazy was hauling Bernice through mud and trees and grasses against her will. But Bernice figured she had to try anyway, even if only to keep the old lady's mind occupied on conversation instead of on whatever creepy thing she was planning on doing. Was she going to kill Bernice? Sure she said she didn't kill, but what if she tied her to a tree stump or something and let dehydration kill her instead? Or she'd knock Bernice over the head and leave her in a puddle of water, and say the swamp had let her drown. Or maybe death didn't mean the same thing to the old lady that it meant to Bernice; maybe dying and turning into organic material to feed the animals and the roots of the swamp plants was not death but eternal life. That didn't seem outside the realm of possibility for this crazy old broad. So Bernice really wanted to keep her talking. Unfortunately, Swamp wasn't the best conversationalist, so Bernice ended up doing most of the talking, and thus couldn't really devote much brain power to trying to plot her escape. "Right? You're the swamp so you know what the swamp decides."

"When the swamp decides, I will know."

"But you're the swamp!"

"Does your hand know what your mind is contemplating?"

"Uh, so you're the swamp's hand?"

"Yes. Its hand," Swamp said approvingly, clearly thinking Bernice was finally catching on. Bernice disagreed. "The swamp needs an ambassador. A hand. And I am getting old. Hence the need for you."

"I can be plenty helpful to the swamp back at the university. Or doing my research. I don't need to see any secrets and I don't need to be dragged anywhere."

Swamp didn't answer.

"So you're the swamp, but you're also … not? Like you don't know what its thinking? Then how—"

"I do not know what the swamp thinks, unless it tells me. Your hand does not know what your mind is contemplating unless your mind needs it to do something. Your mind tells your hand to scratch and itch, and your hand does it. Your mind tells your hand to swat a mosquito, and it does it. Your mind—"

"I get it. Are you aware that you're insane?"

The old lady didn't respond.

Bernice really wished there was some smooth way to segue any of this craziness into a nice, convincing invitation for the old woman to come with Bernice to the homeless shelter downtown. But with each step deeper into the swamp that she was dragged, the very notion that she had thought the homeless shelter idea might work felt more and more stupid. "I know you're Rebecca Hallett," Bernice said.

Again, the old lady didn't respond. But Bernice was pretty sure she felt a tremor in the woman's hand that gripped her wrist.

"You disappeared into this swamp like five or six decades ago." With her free hand, Bernice swatted at more mosquitos. So many mosquitos.

Silence from the old lady.

"You can't be the swamp's hand. You're Rebecca Hallett. A human being who was born outside this swamp and just got lost in here one day and went bonkers from being alone for years drinking filthy swamp water and eating raw birds and licking toads or whatever passes for entertainment out here."

"I was Rebecca Hallet. I became the swamp's hand when I was shown the secret of the swamp by my predecessor."

Bernice felt a chill. Predecessor? Some person had done to Swamp what Swamp was about to try to do to her? "And that would be the same secret of the swamp that you're about to show me?"

"The very same."

"Uh." This was not cool. This secret of the swamp sounded like something Bernice absolutely did not want to see. "What if I don't want to see it?"

"I told you if you came back I'd show you. You came back. So I am showing you."

"I don't want to see it. I want to leave." Though Bernice was trying to sound calm, a definite edge of panic was showing through in her voice.

"Fear not. If the swamp does not choose you, it will let you go. And if it does choose you, you will understand, and you will not want to leave. Either way, you will be fine. Either way, the outcome will feel right."

Bernice didn't answer. If this secret of the swamp had played any part in Rebecca losing her mind, Bernice didn't want anything to do with it. It was probably a mass grave or an illegal dump site full of creepy mind-altering chemicals from a 1960's lab experiment.

Maybe struggling was worth a try after all.

As Rebecca led Bernice past a willow, Bernice grabbed around the trunk with her free arm and held tight, then wrapped one leg around it as well. She braced herself for the inevitable tug when Rebecca kept on walking. When it came, it was nearly enough to rip her free of the tree. But she managed to hold on.

Rebecca turned around to glare at her, and gave her another hard tug that nearly peeled her from the tree trunk. "Come," Rebecca demanded.

"No."

"Come." Tug.

"No. I have no interest at all in seeing the secret of the swamp. I only came here because, uh …" Bernice paused. This was not the way she'd have liked to bring up the idea of the homeless shelter. But a natural segue was just not happening. "Aren't you tired of living out here? Like in the winter and in the heat of the summer and in the rain and all that? Ouch!" she gasped as Swamp tugged hard. "Uh, like you gotta be tired of, um, sleeping on the ground? Getting sunburn? Frostbite?"

Rebecca gave her another tug, and didn't answer.

"Of course you're tired," Bernice answered for her. "Of course you are.

 40

There's this nice place downtown where you can live. It's got heat and air conditioning and clean water and good food, and you can live there, and I can take you there. We can go right now. Sound nice? That's why I'm here. I'm not here to see the secret of the swamp. I'm here to take you to this super nice place where you can be clean and dry and comfortable."

The old woman turned away from her, looking around. "We are nearly there, anyway. This is far enough." Then, she began to search the ground with her eyes.

"What are you looking for?" Bernice asked warily. "Is the secret of the swamp like lying on the ground or something?"

"I am not looking for the secret of the swamp. I am looking for something to hold you still while the swamp works. Ah, there," she said as she spotted something in the grass. "Perfect." Rebecca snapped her fingers.

At first Bernice thought it was a snake. But it was a vine. Moving. Again. Bernice screamed. An Asiatic bittersweet vine was winding its way through some swamp grass toward Bernice. Just like what had happened to Kevin earlier. No matter how many times Bernice saw this moving vine trick of Swamp's, it would never be any less brain-jarring. Rebecca had snapped her fingers and now the plant was moving. Bernice stared in horror at the old woman. Then she glanced back at the vine. This was not happening. This was not possible.

She screamed again. Rebecca didn't even try to stop her screams, which was distressing since it meant the old woman was confident Bernice wouldn't be heard.

The vine was moving all by itself. Closer and closer to her. Rebecca could do ... what? Magic? Telekinesis? Was Bernice hallucinating? This couldn't be real.

Rebecca was now holding Bernice to the tree instead of trying to pull her off of it. The old woman was watching the vine with an intensity that gave Bernice the distinct impression she was not just watching but directing its progress. The vine was creeping up the tree, wrapping around Bernice's ankles, snaking higher and higher until it was wrapped around her entire body. Great. Just great. Asiatic bittersweet had always been high on Bernice's list of most hated invasive species, but this had moved it right to the top of the list. Number one. No question.

Bernice couldn't move. Not an inch. She screamed again.

Rebecca snapped her fingers and the end of the vine slid its way across Bernice's mouth.

Then, as Bernice stared in wide-eyed horror, Rebecca reached into her filthy clothing, brought her hand out in a fist, opened her hand palm upward, and blew some powder into Bernice's face.

CHAPTER SEVEN:

POSTER

BERNICE BEGAN TO gag against the vine in her mouth as the powder entered her lungs.

Rebecca snapped her fingers again and the vine left Bernice's mouth.

"What was that stuff?" Bernice gasped between coughs. None of this was possible. No. She struggled against the vines. The rough bark rubbed against her skin, and didn't give a fraction of an inch.

Rebecca tilted her head to the side, studying Bernice. "Spores and pollen ... and a few other ingredients. I will teach you the concoction if you are deemed worthy," she explained. "You will be fine. Do not be afraid. The swamp will take care of you."

"Let me go! Is this what you did to Kevin?" She thought of his blue lips and crazy giggling. "Is this the secret of—"

"No. This is not the secret of the swamp. The concoction will make your mind a hospitable place for the swamp in the event that it chooses you."

Bernice whimpered, "I need to get out of here. You can't—"

"Be calm. For a while, things will be confusing. But then everything will be clear."

"Confusing? Confusing how?" Bernice asked, panicked, trying to prepare for whatever was about to happen even as she felt something weird going on inside of her head. Some sort of disconnected fogginess was seeping in.

"Things won't be real for a time. You will experience things that seem real but aren't. Then, if you are chosen, you will awaken reborn."

"Not real? Wh-what do you—" Bernice asked, blinking against the weird feeling in her eyes. "Reborn? Seriously, let me go. This is—"

"I cannot say in what way things will not be real for you. For me, I was an activist working for civil rights. Eventually I was elected president."

Bernice shook her head. Rebecca was still talking, but the disconnected fogginess was pressing against the back of her eyes and her ears were ringing and she couldn't hear, and then she could hear because she heard herself giggling. Oh shoot. Giggling. Like Kevin. She tried to hold on to normalcy, but normalcy melted right away out of her brain into the air and everything was hilarious and Rebecca disappeared in a puff of smoke. Had that really happened? Probably not. Swamp presidents. People or swamps disappearing in puffs of smoke or puffs of spores or pollen or whatever. It didn't matter. It was hilarious. Everything was hilarious.

Until the ringing in her ears started.

Louder and louder and louder and she wanted to scream except that would have made things even louder and she couldn't take any more loudness. Her head was going to explode.

Everything got blindingly bright.

Then blackness.

Bernice woke slowly to the sound of a red-winged blackbird singing in the tree above her head. Why had she never noticed before how grating the call of the red-winged blackbird was? Why had she never noticed before how bright the world was? She could barely open her eyes. She heard a voice. She heard a low, relentless ringing, quiet, almost not there, but definitely constant.

"Huh?" she croaked, blinking. She opened her eyes a crack. There was a person standing a few yards away from her. A man.

"Hey, kid, you okay?"

"Huh?" she repeated. Wow, her throat was dry. She was thirsty. So thirsty. And that ringing was irritating. And everything was weird. Foggy. Heavy. Her eyes felt strange.

The guy laughed. "Are you okay?" He sounded familiar. Her eyes were slowly adjusting. She could tell he was tall and had short, dark hair. A green jacket. Why was he wearing a jacket in this heat?

"Who are you?"

"What are you doing stuck to that tree?" the guy questioned as he took a few steps closer.

Stuck to a tree? Huh? She opened her eyes a bit more and looked around. Why was she in the swamp? Why had she been unconscious in the swamp? There were vines wrapped around her. Asiatic bittersweet by the look of them. She was being held vertical to a tree by a long vine of Asiatic bittersweet. She wiggled around a bit. It was pretty loose. She could get out, easy. "Can you give me a hand?" she asked as she started pushing against the vines. The vines were by no means tight, but they were hard to bend.

The guy stepped closer.

Bernice pushed against the top vine, and the end of it unwrapped from around the willow behind her. She did the same to the second coil and the third, all the while wondering why this guy was not helping her. He was just standing there silently, watching her struggle. "Come on, dude, give me a hand," she said.

"Have you seen anyone else in these parts?" he asked her.

"Uh. No. No, I just woke up a minute ago stuck to a tree. I haven't seen anyone but you," she replied as she pushed against the fourth coil. It was too thick, too securely wrapped around the tree behind her. But it and the coils below it were loose enough for her to wriggle around. She looked up at the willow branches above her head. She grabbed one and pulled herself up about a foot, then used the coils as a sort of ladder, climbing upward and over the spiral of vine. Pulling herself up as much as she could, she squirmed over so she was hanging from the branch, outside the vines. She let go and landed on her feet, free from the bittersweet. How on earth had she gotten there? What was going on? She looked over at the unhelpful man. Her eyes widened. She recognized him. Oh wow. Bernice squeaked, "Captain Joe?"

He grinned and did a mock bow. "I see my reputation precedes me. I'm surprised a person on this little backwater rock knows who I am!"

"Of course I know who you are!" she breathed. "I have a post—" Bernice stopped short. Oops. Play it cool, Bernice. Don't mention the poster of

Captain Joe on your bedroom wall. You're twenty-four. There's no excuse.

"Uh … I have a post … a post—"

"You're posted here?" he asked.

Bernice grabbed the lifeline. "Yes. Yes. That's it. Yup, I'm posted here."

"Oh! Well that explains it." He flashed a crooked grin. "How long has Central had you out here?"

"Uh. I've been posted here for three months."

"Doing what?" Captain Joe asked, looking around bemusedly. "Sitting around watching birds?"

"Um."

"Where's your base?"

"Uh …"

"Kid, you okay?"

"Uh, I'm super thirsty. My ears are ringing." She shook her head. "You got any water?"

"Not on me. There's some on the ship." There was a blinding flash of white light, and for a second Captain Joe disappeared. She was standing alone in the swamp and it was the middle of the night. Her stomach hurt. She felt like she was going to vomit. A crescent moon shone down straight overhead. Midnight? What? Another flash a few seconds later, and it was daytime again, and Captain Joe was back. Her stomach felt fine.

Bernice blinked. "What just happened?"

"What do you mean?" asked Captain Joe.

"You just … uh …" She shook her head. "Never mind." Weird.

"Okay, kid … if you're sure …" He did a classic Captain Joe eyebrow lift and head tilt. "So, like I was saying … let's head back to the Mantis."

The Mantis. That snapped Bernice out of her preoccupation. She gasped and stared at him. The ship! Oh wow. "Is the whole crew here?" she asked giddily.

He nodded. "Yep. Zed, our pilot, his brain got infected by this parasite. It—"

Bernice gasped. She had just watched this episode two nights ago! She cut in enthusiastically, "Oh yeah! It infected his brain and made him fly to—Oh, wow—" The parasite made him fly to Earth? Wow. That did not seem quite right. But here Captain Joe was. So clearly she'd gotten it wrong. Her head was so foggy. "The parasite brought you to Earth."

"Ah," said Captain Joe. "I see Central is keeping you abreast of our developments. Let's go to your post. We need some parts for our engine. I bet you've got spares. They're standard. Central will have equipped you."

"Oh, uh. I …" Bernice muttered, putting a hand to her incessantly ringing head. "I don't have any spare anything. A Darra raiding party came through a month back. I've got nothing."

Captain Joe raised his eyebrows. "Darra all the way out here on the outskirts?"

"Yup." Please believe it, Captain.

"Aw shoot. Well, okay. Marcus will manage something. Let's head back to the ship."

Bernice could barely conceal her glee. Captain Joe was taking her to the Space Mantis! And Marcus was there! Beautiful, beautiful Marcus the mechanic, who always managed to find a reason to take his shirt off at least once an episode. Oh, swoon. Marcus was—as of the end of the most recent season—single, since Salia had turned out to be a double agent who had been using him in order to spy on the crew of the Mantis for General Waters. Yes. Marcus was single. And, as luck would have it, Bernice was single, too. She and Marcus had so much in common. They were both in their 20's, and they both had black hair, and … uh, whatever. Match made in heaven.

Bernice fell into step beside Captain Joe. The ringing was getting louder. Very irritating. But she tried to ignore it, since there she was talking to the captain of the Space Mantis. She didn't want to ruin the moment by talking about a ringing sound in her ears. He'd probably think she had a parasite in her brain like how Zed did. Wait, what if she did have a parasite in her brain like how Zed did? If the parasite had brought them to Earth, did that mean the parasites originated on Earth? That made sense. Otherwise, how would the parasite have known about Earth? Oh shoot. Did she have a parasite? Were they going to quarantine her? How could she put the moves on Marcus the mechanic if she was locked away in the sick bay with no one but the hard-as-nails Dr. Angela for company? She really didn't want that parasite. It had nearly killed Zed. But she was probably just dehydrated. That was all it was. Not the parasite. Nope. "How far until we reach the Mantis?" she asked Captain Joe.

"It's just up ahead. Zed crashed us right in—" Captain Joe stopped short and directed his gaze to the sky. "You hear that?"

"I …" Bernice said. "No … I don't hear anything …" But then she heard it. The screaming of a Darra raider. Or was that the ringing in her head?

Captain Joe said, "Quick! Take cover! Over here!" He signaled her toward a tree.

She ran after him.

A woman yelled from behind them, "Captain! Wait up!"

Captain Joe looked over his shoulder as he ran. Bernice looked, too. Infiniti, the ship's cyborg, was running after them toting some sort of super huge gun thing over her shoulder as though it weighed nothing. While Infiniti ran and dodged tree branches, she shot the captain a smoldering, flirty look that was totally inappropriate considering that a Darra raider was skimming the treetops behind her, spraying bullets in her direction. She glanced over her shoulder at the raider, halted, swung the big gun into position, and shot the raider out of the sky with one resounding blast. As it sputtered and drifted off course, heading toward the ground, Infiniti turned back to them. The mischievous wink she shot the captain was perfectly choreographed with the fiery crash of the raider as it hit the ground in the near distance. The flames of the burning ship cast an orange glow on her perfectly sculpted blonde hair.

Bernice gaped. Infiniti was so cool. She wondered if Captain Joe and the cyborg would ever go beyond flirting. They'd be such an awesome couple. But she doubted the captain would ever be able to get past the fact that Infiniti was not technically human.

"Glad you could join the party," Captain Joe said to the cyborg, flashing his crooked grin as a second raider sounded in the distance.

Infiniti slung the gun back up onto her shoulder and was just opening her mouth to give him a response that was probably equal parts witty, flippant, and innuendo-riddled, but just then another blinding flash of light shot through Bernice's skull.

Bernice blinked. Captain Joe was gone. Infiniti was gone. It was daytime. Pouring rain. She was cold. Shivering. She coughed violently. Her stomach muscles had that sore feeling that indicated she'd been coughing for a while. Except she hadn't. Her nose was runny and her head ached. She saw a flash of movement to her left. She looked. Rebecca. Another flash of light. She was huddling behind a tree trunk while Captain Joe shot his laser gun at a low-flying Darra raider. She was not soaking wet, not coughing, no headache.

Infiniti was standing over her with the big gun at the ready, utterly fearless as only a cyborg could be in the face of an onslaught of bullets. It looked like she'd taken a few hits. A hole was blasted in Infiniti's side. Exposed wires were hanging out of the hole. There was another hole in her lower right thigh that Bernice could see through clean to the other side. Looked like Marcus would have his work cut out for him patching her up.

"Come on! Move! Move! Move!" Captain Joe yelled and signaled for them to move from the cover of the tree to another tree a bit farther north.

Bernice swallowed nervously, took a deep breath, then ran, with Captain Joe close at her side, firing at the raider. Infiniti took up the rear.

Once they were safe under the next willow tree, the captain muttered to Bernice, "Where's your gun, anyway?"

"The Darra raiders who took all my extra supplies took my weapons, too," she explained. Thus far, Captain Joe was not questioning why the Darra hadn't just killed her. It seemed like only a matter of time until it occurred to him.

"Why didn't they just kill you?" Captain Joe suddenly asked with a suspicious eyebrow raise.

Shoot! "Uh, I ran away. Hid."

"Hmm." Narrowing his eyes, he studied her. Oh, no. He was looking skeptical. He was catching her lying vibes and misinterpreting them. She was not his enemy! She was like his biggest fan!

"Captain, I promise you—" The ringing in her ears intensified. She shook her head. Again, a bright flash of light. The half-light of early morning or late evening. She was trudging through the swamp. She was freezing cold. Snow was falling from the steel gray sky. Snow? How on earth was it snowing? It was the middle of the summer. Something yellow flapped by a leafless tree ahead of her. Her first thought was of a goldfinch, but this was winter. The yellow was not a bird. As her teeth chattered, she squinted at the yellow. It looked like ... police tape? A bit of police tape hanging loose in a tree? She got closer, reached out—

The bright flash of light brought her back to Captain Joe.

She was on her back, staring up at the ceiling of a well-lit room.

A voice across the room said, "Ah, you're awake."

Bernice turned toward the voice. Dr. Angela was standing at a counter, drawing some medicine out of a bottle with a huge syringe. Bernice stared at the syringe. That had better not be for her. "What am I doing here?" she gasped. "How'd I get—"

"You came with the captain. Don't you remember?" Dr. Angela asked. She narrowed her eyes at Bernice, set down the bottle, and walked over with the syringe in her hand. She stopped by the bed Bernice was lying in and put a hand to her forehead. "Before you fell asleep, we had a conversation. Don't you remember that?"

Bernice shook her head slowly and swallowed. What was going on?

"You were telling me about the Darra that attacked you and stole all your stuff. You remember none of that?" Dr. Angela asked as she held Bernice's left eye open and examined it with a little penlight. She did the same to Bernice's right eye, then sighed.

Bernice said, "No. I don't remember a thing."

Dr. Angela picked the syringe up and tapped the needle. "Okay. Interesting. Well, don't worry. You're in good hands."

Bernice barely heard her words. She was too busy staring in horror at the huge syringe. "What is that?" she whispered.

"All-in-one vaccine," Dr. Angela explained, giving her a quizzical look. "You've never had one? The captain said you were with Central."

Of course. The all-in-one. The doctor was always giving new people on the ship this vaccine. They traveled all over the galaxy getting exposed to all sorts of germs, and this vaccine was a cocktail of vaccines of as many of the diseases as Central was able to manage. People like Bernice who had not been exposed to many of them needed the vaccine in case the Mantis was carrying something weird from across the galaxy. "Of course," Bernice said. "The vaccine. I … you see, the syringe is just so much bigger in real life—"

"In real life?" Dr. Angela asked, grabbing Bernice's arm and straightening it.

"Uh … Bernice began to squirm. She hated needles. Her body began fighting Dr. Angela before her brain even realized she was doing it.

"Hold still," Dr. Angela snapped.

"Wait."

"This is essential. You know it is," Dr. Angela panted as she tried to hold Bernice down. "Geez, kid, if I didn't know better, I'd think you'd never had one before."

Bernice twisted her arm out of the doctor's grip.

Dr. Angela shot her a glare and hit the nearby intercom on the wall. "I need some muscle in the sick bay, Marcus."

Even through her needle-induced panic, Bernice's heart leapt. Marcus! She looked at the sick bay door—the ringing in her head went crazy. No, not now! Not now

A bright flash of light brought her to the swamp. She was lying on her back, staring at the starry night sky. She was chilly, but not the intense winter cold of before. It was almost soothing. Especially with the cool softness of the moss beneath her. She smiled contentedly. Everything was so peaceful. A bug crawled out of her hair and across her face. She held still so as not to startle it. Another bright flash brought her back to the Mantis. She was sitting on a cot in the brig, looking through the bars to the dark hall beyond. Oh no. What on earth? She was in the brig! What had happened?

And the ship was moving. She glanced through the tiny sliver of a window on the wall behind her. Stars. She was in space. Where were they going? What was going on?

Down the dark hall, a door opened and footsteps approached. She stood and walked to the bars. "Hey!" she yelled. "What's going on!?"

From the shadows and into the dim light of the bulb outside her cell, Marcus appeared.

Her heart fluttered. He was even more handsome in real life. He gave her a sparkly grin that conveyed a confusing degree of familiarity. Did he know her? "Hey sweetheart," he said. "He's not budging. I tried, but no dice." He halted on the opposite side of the bars, reached through, and put a hand to the side of her face. "But don't worry. He'll see sense. The captain always sees sense in the end." He brushed his thumb across her lips.

Bernice stared at him with wide eyes. Oh. Oh wow. What? She and Marcus? Huh? Were they together? Why did she not have those memories? She needed those memories. "Uh."

"At the very least, once the baby comes there's no way he'll make you stay in here—"

Bernice gaped at him, then looked down at her stomach. She screamed. She was pregnant. She screamed again. She looked wildly at Marcus, who was staring at her with utter confusion. She saw a tattoo on his hand. The swoopy tattoo that his people got when they got married. She glanced down at her hand. She had a matching tattoo. They were married and she was pregnant and what on earth was going on?

"Honey!" Marcus gasped. "Bernice! Calm down—"

"Don't tell me to calm down!" she screeched. "I—"

The ever-present ringing got loud. Louder. Louder. She doubled over, fell to the ground, put her hands to her ears. It hurt. It was too loud. Her head was going to explode. The brightest flash yet exploded before her eyes.

Silence.

Well, not silence, but a blessed absence of ringing. Birdsong. A swamp sparrow, a red-winged blackbird, and some sort of warbler. She'd never been great at warblers. All over her body, she was aware of tiny little pinpricks of pain. Not horrible by any means, but very present and very constant. She opened her eyes, blinked, and shut her eyes against the brightness. It felt like her eyes had been shut for ages. She was lying on the ground in the swamp. It was hot. She felt the ground on either side of her. Moss, covered in an inch or so of water. She was soaking wet. Her hand flew to her stomach. No baby. Phew. Weird. Very weird. As her hand moved to her stomach, she brushed against some plants. She felt them. Grasses and vines were bent over her body. She opened her eyes a crack and looked down. They were not just bent over her body. Vines were actually growing over her body. Trailing plants had crept over her, and her clothing was muddy. Filthy. Unrecognizable.

She sat bolt upright and convulsively fought free of the plants that had grown over her. Her breath came in short gasps as she jumped to her feet. Her legs gave way beneath her and she splashed into the mud. Her muscles felt weak, unable to support her body. Her gaze bounced wildly around the swamp. She couldn't breathe. Was she having a panic attack? Very likely, all things considered. Very, very likely. She let out an incoherent scream because it felt like the best possible way to express her emotion at that moment, and her voice came out in a hoarse rasp.

A few yards away, there was movement from the grasses. The old woman—Rebecca—sat up from where she'd apparently been lying in the mud. As Bernice gaped in horror at her and tried to get to her feet, Rebecca smiled and said, "At last. You've awoken. How do you feel?"

Bernice rasped, "What is going on?"

Rebecca held her hands up before her soothingly. "You are confused. You need to lie down. Rest. I will explain—"

Bernice managed to stand. She staggered backward, tripped on a root, and nearly fell again. "No!"

"You will harm yourself if you move too much after emerging—"

"Shut up!" Bernice screeched.

"You need to sit down."

"No! No, I do not! I need to get out of here!"

The old woman sighed and nodded. "Do what you must. I will be here when you return. I will find you."

"Whatever," Bernice mumbled. "You crazy old freak. Whatever. I am out of here. I am never setting foot in this place again." Bernice wobbled away. She had no idea which direction was which and she didn't care. If she kept on walking, she'd eventually reach the edge of the swamp, and that was all that mattered. She was done. This was insane. She was dropping her plans to get a master's in ecology. She was going to get a job at the gas station by her apartment and she was never looking back. As she tripped away, she glanced back at Rebecca. The old woman was sitting in the mud watching her with a knowing sort of expression.

Bernice ran her hands through her hair. Or tried to. Her fingers got stuck in the mass of knots and plant matter. So tangled she couldn't move her fingers through it.

Her hands started to shake. Her legs started to shake. Her whole body started to shake as her panic totally enveloped her.

How long had she been in the swamp?

What had happened to her?

CHAPTER EIGHT:

EVERYTHING IS FINE. EVERYTHING IS FINE. EVERYTHING IS FINE.

BERNICE STARED OUT the hospital window at the view of the park three floors down. As she stared, she listened to her doctor and a police officer talking low in the hallway. They'd been going back and forth for a few minutes. She was glad she had their conversation to listen to since it took her mind off the nagging feeling in her mind that she had to get back to the swamp. Since the moment she'd woken in the hospital bed, she had been aware of an irritating voice in the back of her mind insisting that she needed to return. She was trying to chalk it up to irrational anxiety—knowing that she'd lost a year of her life and a year of her work, and that her plans of getting a master's were probably derailed and that her life was in shambles. Yes. That was it. That explained the nagging voice in the back of her head. Just anxiety about a lost year of life.

Never mind that this voice in the back of her head was not at all the form of anxiety she was used to. Her usual anxiety was borderline-obsessive feelings of stress and worry, not an actual voice whispering repeatedly, *Come back to the swamp, come back to the swamp.*

So, yes, she was glad she was able to focus on the conversation in the hall. Anything that kept her mind off the voice was welcome.

The doctor was saying, "I'm telling you, I don't think she's up to visitors yet, Officer."

"But the sooner we get information from her, the sooner we can get back into that swamp and—"

"I'm afraid I must insist," the doctor stated in a very firm voice.

The cop grumbled, "Fine. Fine. You give me a call the minute she's able to talk."

Bernice sighed, and called, "I can talk to you, Officer!" Talking to the cop would be an even better way of blocking out the voice.

Come back to the swamp, come back to the swamp.

The men stopped short, and a moment later they both appeared in the doorway. While the officer strode in with an expression of concern on his face, the doctor hung back, frowning disapprovingly.

The officer halted beside Bernice's bed and said, "Thank you, Ms. Martin. You sure you're up to talking?"

"Yep," Bernice said, keeping it short since talking felt weird. Her vocal cords hadn't been used much the past year. One year. She'd been missing in the swamp almost an entire year, wandering around hallucinating about the crew of the Space Mantis. It had felt like an hour at most. But a year of her life was gone, lost to temporary insanity brought on by whatever that horrible old woman had done to her. Her mind wouldn't quite let her think about it too much. Every time she wondered too hard about it, her mind put up a wall. She didn't push too hard. Her mind knew what it was doing.

The officer smiled and nodded. "Great. I gotta say, I'm thrilled you were found. I've been on this case since day one. It's so nice when these missing persons cases end well. Do you have any idea where you were kept? The doctor says you don't remember anything. We searched every inch of that swamp multiple times. Do you have any idea whether you were there the whole time?"

"I dunno," Bernice answered with a shrug. She cleared her throat. "I mean, I remember bits and pieces. But that's it. Walking around in the night. Walking around in the rain. And in the snow. Lying in some moss. That's about it."

"Every one of your memories is in the swamp? Never anywhere else?"

"Never anywhere else." *Come back to the swamp, come back to the swamp.* Bernice gave her head a sharp shake.

He nodded, wrote some stuff in his notebook, and tapped his pen against his chin, thinking. "Uh, this old lady. The cops who responded to the call from the person who found you by the roadside, they mentioned you'd said something about an old lady."

Bernice nodded. She whispered in a rush, "Yes. Rebecca Hallett. I asked her if she was and she said yes. Or, rather, she said she had been Rebecca Hallett but that now she is the swamp. Because she's insane. She's totally insane." Bernice's throat felt so weird. Tired from all this talking. But now that she'd started she couldn't stop. She had too much to say. And talking helped drown out the voice. *Come back to the swamp, come back to the swamp.* "She ranted about being the swamp and she blew drugs in my face and then everything went crazy and that's when I lost a year of my life and— Oh! Hey! Kevin James! What happened to him? Is he alive? Did she kill him? Please tell me Kevin's alive."

"Kevin James …" murmured the cop, tapping his pen against his chin again as he gave Bernice a funny look. "Uh, yeah, he was the one who first reported you missing."

Bernice exhaled a relieved breath. She had been fairly convinced he was dead. "Was he missing long himself?" she asked. *Come back to the swamp, come back to the swamp.*

"Uh, no …" the cop said, for some reason confused by the question. "No, he called us the morning after you disappeared. Called from the swamp. On your phone."

"Wait. He was okay? The old lady blew the same drugs in his face that she did mine …" Why had she lost an entire year and Kevin had only been out a night? Had the old lady been dosing her over and over, day after day? The thought made her sick and scared—her wandering around out of her senses and lost, with horrible old Rebecca Hallett continually drugging her.

"Yeah he was okay except a broken ankle." He frowned. "Why? Do you have anything to report about Mr. James?"

Bernice raised an eyebrow. "Anything to report? What do you mean?"

The doctor cut in, looking at the monitors she was hooked up to, "If you wouldn't mind, Officer, I'd like you to wrap this up. The stress she's undergone—"

"Yes," the officer said, not turning to the doctor. "Yes, of course. Ms. Martin. I know you don't have many memories. But is there anything you can tell me that might help us pinpoint this woman? Any landmarks you recall? Anything she said?"

"Um …" Bernice stared out the window, thinking. *Come back to the swamp, come back to the swamp.* Well, there was the alarming fact that Rebecca did seem to show up, raving about being in pain, whenever a branch was cut in the swamp. Unless she was in her hibernation state. But no way was Bernice going to tell the cop any of that. She wanted to keep all that insanity under wraps. She didn't want anyone thinking she was crazy. She was not crazy. Nope. All the weirdness could be explained by drugs. The time loss, imagining the *Space Mantis* cast, the voice—yes, somehow the voice that was playing on repeat in her head over and over nonstop was just a residual drug thing. "Uh, well I did see her most frequently in the research plot. But I don't think that really means anything. Doesn't mean she hung out there frequently. Just that I did. Ya know?"

He nodded. "Yeah. Sure." But he wrote something down anyway.

While he wrote, the room filled with silence and the voice in her head got even more annoying. "I'll let you know if I think of something else," she rasped to fill the silence. "Something is bound to come to mind."

The cop frowned at his notebook. She was not giving him much to go on.

"Oh," she said. "If you get me an aerial photo or a topo map or something I can show you the approximate place I was when I … uh, snapped out of whatever she'd done to me. She was with me when I woke up. Maybe you can find something there. Since she was there. Ya know?" Wow, her throat was sore. Bernice continued, "Like maybe she left behind some footprints in the mud or whatever. But would footprints be much help to you? I bet since you probably found footprints when you were searching the swamp before for me and that never got me found—"

"Great," the cop cut in, standing up. "Yeah, I'll get you those maps. That'd be great if you could pinpoint that location to the best of your ability. And if you're able to circle any other spots you think you might remember being, that'd be great, too."

She cleared her tired throat. "Sure. Happy to help. I really want to do anything I can to help you get that old woman. If I think of anything else I'll let you know. I—"

"Thanks, Ms. Martin. I'll send someone over with those maps. You get some rest."

"Thanks, Officer," Bernice said. As he walked out, she turned to the doctor. She needed to start a conversation with him. *Come back to the swamp, come back to the swamp.* "Any word on my blood tests?"

The doctor shook his head. "Nothing conclusive yet."

"Oh," Bernice sighed. She really wanted to get those results. She was hoping like crazy they'd find some sort of official results involving crazy hallucinogenic mushroom spores. Something that would give her solid proof that everything weird she'd seen and experienced could be explained away by drugs and not anything supernatural. It would take some doing for her to convince herself that those moving vines had only been a hallucination, but if she wanted denial strongly enough she was sure her brain would help her out.

The doctor walked over to her, checked her vitals, and instructed, "Get some rest, Bernice. Is there anything else you need?"

"Yeah, could I get a TV in here?"

"You need your rest, Bernice. You'll have plenty of time to catch up on TV later. Get a good night of sleep, and then we can have a TV brought in tomorrow morning."

Bernice swallowed. She needed background noise. *Come back to the swamp, come back to the swamp.* "I need a TV," she demanded, her voice wavering weirdly. "Or a radio. Something. Some sound. I really just need it."

The doctor narrowed his eyes and studied her. "Is something wrong?" His eyes flicked back to the monitor at Bernice's bedside and he watched the visual evidence of her elevated heart rate.

"No. I just … I'm fine. Just can I get a TV?" she asked, cringing at the panic in her voice that she could do nothing to disguise. She was not crazy. Everything was fine. Everything was fine.

"Sure, Bernice. Sure. If it's that important to you, sure," he said soothingly. "I'll have a nurse bring one in."

"Thank you," she exclaimed, her gratefulness excessively heartfelt for the circumstances.

The doctor raised an eyebrow, studied her face for clues about her weird behavior, and said, "I'll check in on you later."

"Thanks."

"Rest," he said, walking toward the door.

Once he'd gone, she began to whisper, "The sun was shining on the sea, shining with all his might. He did his very best to make the billows smooth and bright. And this was odd because it was the middle of the night ..."

CHAPTER NINE:

THE VOICE

MAYBE BERNICE SHOULDN'T have screamed at her nurses, ripped her IV out, and checked herself out of the hospital against her doctor's wishes. But the nurses had insisted on making Bernice turn off the TV that night, so she had had to leave. She needed the TV. She needed it loud. She needed to stop the voice. And she couldn't explain it to them. They'd just think she was crazy. And she wasn't. All she was was stressed out. Anxious. Maybe she should have told them about the voice. Maybe. But no. She could probably get locked up at a mental hospital for that kind of thing, and if she got locked up then she couldn't leave and go to the swamp. Not that she was going to go to the swamp. She wasn't going to listen to the voice. It wasn't a real thing. It wasn't the swamp calling to her. It was anxiety. She just needed to block it out, get it out of her head, calm down, quit this downward spiral of anxiety. The stress was feeding on itself, getting worse and worse. If she could just chill out and breathe and get some distraction, she'd be able to break the cycle and the voice would go away and everything would be fine.

Everything would be fine.

It felt strange to be showered and wearing brand new clothes. Everything felt foreign. At least she had her old backpack that the cops had gotten out of evidence for her. She strode through the hospital lobby and out into the warm night air. She took a deep breath. The humidity was strangely soothing. She used to hate humidity. But that had been before the swamp. She supposed her body had just grown accustomed to living without air conditioning in the past year.

She welcomed the sounds of the cars driving down the road. The voice was fairly easy to block out with all the background noise of civilization.

Before checking out, Bernice had nearly called a friend for a ride, but she didn't feel up to the pity or the curiosity or the awkwardness. Her friend and old freshman roommate, Kate, had tried to visit her in the hospital, but Bernice had been all too happy to use her doctor's excuse of needing rest. She could do reunions later. Right now, the idea of a conversation with a pitying, morbidly curious person was so horrible that she wanted to avoid it even more than she wanted distraction from the voice.

She pulled a printout out of the front pocket of her backpack—some people at the hospital had given her a list of hotels she could stay at free of charge; some charity or something had heard about her situation and had sent over some resources for her, saying something about how since she had no family they wanted to help her get on her feet after her ordeal. Once Bernice had her life together a bit more, she intended to write an epic thank you note for the hotel options, the new cell phone, the new clothes, and the rather huge amount of money.

It was weird to think that her apartment had long ago been rented by someone else and that all her stuff was in storage. It was a very disconnected feeling, having no place or stuff of her own. Not even her own clothes. At least she had her backpack. It still had mud crusted on it from the swamp, which made her oddly happy.

She spotted a taxi and was about to hail it when she heard a guy yell, "Hey, Bernice! B!"

She spotted him running down the sidewalk toward her from the hospital parking lot. She squinted through the semi-dark of the late evening. "Kevin?" she gasped. She waited for him to trot the rest of the way up to where she stood. He'd cut his hair short, and shaved his beard. His khakis and nondescript blue button-up shirt were not at all the usual art-slacker Kevin attire. "What the heck?" Bernice asked, gesturing to his getup and his clean-shaven face when he halted in front of her.

He didn't answer her, but just said, "Wow," staring at her. He exhaled a steadying breath. "It's really you. I had to see for myself. You have no idea how good it is to see you alive, B." He really did sound very happy. There was something in his voice—a desperate sort of relief—that confused her.

"Yeah. Same here, man. I was sure that old lady killed you with that stuff she blew in your face." How strange that, for him, an entire year had passed, but for her it felt like almost no time at all.

He was still staring at her with that agitated, intense relief.

Come back to the swamp, come back to the swamp.

He shrugged aside the mention of the old lady. "Oh, that? Man, that was nothing compared to what happened next."

Bernice felt a spike of rage toward Rebecca. "What— Did she find you later and do something to you?" she hissed.

He blinked. "Um, no."

"What then?" Bernice asked.

He swallowed, his gaze dancing around nervously. "No one told you?"

She narrowed her eyes. "Uh …"

He cleared his throat. "B, they thought I murdered you."

"What?" Bernice screeched. "They *what?*"

Kevin ran shaking hands through his now-short hair. "Yep."

Bernice spluttered incoherently.

Kevin nodded in agreement.

"No way," she breathed. "No. Like did you go to *jail?*"

Kevin nodded. "Yeah, for a while. But they couldn't find any evidence— obviously—so they had to let me go. I'd probably still be there if I weren't rich and white. But, still, no one believed me. Rich whiteness couldn't get me that far," he said with a bleak laugh. "And of course I couldn't tell them what really happened or they'd think I was—" He broke off and looked around as though he'd forgotten until that moment that they were standing in front of the door to the lobby of the hospital. "You got somewhere to be? I can drive you. You got a car? Wanna go somewhere and talk?" Bernice could see he was really eager to talk. Poor guy must have been going nuts the past year with no one to talk to about what had really happened in the swamp. And people though he was a murderer. A murderer. Kevin. Insane. The poor guy.

Bernice had thought she wanted to be alone. But Kevin was different. Kevin would understand stuff. Kevin had seen Rebecca snap her fingers and make a vine come to life ... except of course vines were already alive. But Rebecca had made it move. And Kevin had seen it happen. It had wrapped around his wrists and held him in place while she'd blown creepy drugs in his face. Thus, he knew Rebecca was ... what? Magic? A witch? What? "Yeah, let's go somewhere." *Come back to the swamp, come back to the swamp.* "Somewhere loud."

Kevin turned up the radio as he steered his car onto the onramp to the expressway. They had opted to just drive around aimlessly while they talked, instead of chatting about insanity and murder accusations over lattes at a coffee shop.

At Bernice's request, Kevin had put the volume of the radio pretty loud, but she turned it up a bit more.

He raised his eyebrows and said loudly over the radio, "That's a commercial for divorce attorneys, B. You pump up strange jams."

"I don't care what it is so long as it's loud," she responded. She couldn't be sure, but she thought the voice was getting louder. She looked over at Kevin, whose eyes were glued to the road. "So ... jail?"

He glanced her way and sighed. "Yep. Jail. I went to jail."

"You went to jail." She shook her head.

He nodded.

"Why? Why did they suspect you? You're so not a murderer."

"Oh man. So many reasons," he replied. "Uh, the camera on the parking lot at the science building caught me getting into your car, and that was the last you were seen on campus or anywhere, and they worked out I was the last person who'd seen you. And then I had your backpack and your phone and your water when they found me in the swamp, and they thought I'd killed you and dumped you in the swamp and taken your stuff. They worked out some crazy story about how I was obsessed with you and you rejected me and I killed you in a jealous rage."

Bernice felt sick. "No. Oh, Kevin ... that's horrible. I'm so sorry."

"B, don't. It's not your fault."

"But I should never have taken you into that swamp. Not after I started suspecting what she was."

"I said don't," he snapped, angrily. "Don't apologize, Bernice."

She stared at him. The Kevin she knew did not get angry like that.

He gave her an apologetic glance, exhaled sharply, and said, "Sorry. Just please don't apologize." He hit the steering wheel with his fist.

Bernice said, "Geez, man, what's up? This isn't you."

"It's been a rough year."

Bernice frowned. "Aw, please don't tell me your cool dude slacker vibe is gone."

He gave a grudging laugh. "It's kinda hard to maintain. It goes in waves."

"You'll get things back on track," Bernice assured. "Everyone knows you're not a murderer now. I mean, here I am. Not dead."

"Yeah." He got quiet.

"You still in that band? The folky band that played that club just off campus?"

"Nah. Concerts got weird after you disappeared. People showed up yelling at me and stuff. I figured it'd be better for the rest of the band if I made myself scarce."

Bernice frowned. "Still painting?"

"Uh, sorta." He gave a forced laugh. "Sorry I'm being so depressing."

"No problem. It is what it is." Bernice turned up the music a bit more and watched the trees and buildings as they sped by. She couldn't hear the voice, but she could feel it. Somehow, she knew it was there.

After a bit, Kevin said over the music, "Just please don't feel guilty. That creepy old lady took you. It's her fault. Not yours. She messed you up and she messed me up and it's all her fault."

Bernice nodded. "You're right."

"Are the cops looking for her?"

"I think so. They asked me questions about her but I couldn't give them much. My memories are sparse. And foggy. Very confused."

He gave a shuddering sigh. "They were all so convinced it was me. Even after they had to let me go, police would park outside my house. What friends I still had told me officers would ask them questions about me. I know they were just doing their job and all, but … I mean, I was innocent. That's why they had no evidence. Because I didn't do it."

Bernice swallowed. Something else occurred to her, and though she didn't want to hear the answer, she asked anyway, "Are you still in school?"

Clenching his teeth, he shook his head. "Couldn't juggle the murder thing and school. No way."

"But now you'll go back, right?"

"I haven't had a chance to think about it, B. Just found out you were back a few hours ago. But sure. Probably." He paused. "Can we talk about you? It's been a hell of a year, but now it's over because here you are not murdered."

"Not murdered at all," she said. It really would be nice to talk to him about it. He would believe her probably. "Sure, let's talk about me."

"It really is so great to see you alive," he repeated. "I mean, I sure knew I didn't kill you, but I figured our pal Rebecca had. Why didn't she? Like what was the point of her taking you? What'd you do out there this past year?"

"No idea," Bernice sighed. "I mostly hallucinated. No idea what she was up to all that time, but it probably involved drugging me repeatedly and making sure I ate food and didn't die."

Kevin looked from the road to her with wide eyes. "That is messed up. Like really messed up. Did they get you a therapist at the hospital?"

"Yeah, I talked to her for a few minutes when they brought me in. I have another appointment tomorrow morning." Thoughts of therapy made her think of the voice she didn't want to talk about and the *Space Mantis* hallucinations she'd had. "Uh, did you see stuff when she blew those spores and stuff in your face?"

"Oh man. Dude, Bernice. That was crazy. I was the lead singer of this sweet Americana band and we toured all over and it was awesome. I only saw it in flashes, but the flashes I saw were amazingly, amazingly awesome."

"Whoa. Fun."

"Yeah. How about you?"

"I was in an episode of *Space Mantis*. Or a season. Or whatever."

"Sweet!"

She laughed. "It was, kinda."

"Silver lining, eh?" Kevin smiled. "Hey, so why do we have the music so loud?"

Bernice glanced out the window and frowned. Well, if she couldn't tell him, she couldn't tell anyone, and it sure would be nice to tell someone. She swallowed and said in a rush, "I've been hearing a voice in my head. It's telling me to go back to the swamp."

"Huh?"

"A voice. In my head."

"Like your imagination?"

"No, Kevin. No. Not my imagination. A voice that's nothing to do with me. In my head."

He turned his gaze from the road to stare at her.

"Yup." She nodded. "Hey, look at the road, will ya?"

After another moment of staring at her concernedly, he did look back at the road. "A voice in your head."

"Please don't think I'm crazy," Bernice begged.

"I don't think you're crazy, B."

"Are you just saying that?"

He shrugged. "Maybe? I dunno. If you are crazy, you sure have good reason to be."

"I don't want to be crazy," she said desperately. Horrible old Rebecca. Had she made Bernice insane? This had to be temporary. It just had to be. She couldn't stand it, this nagging feeling that she needed to go back. She didn't want to go back.

"So the voice is telling you to go back to the swamp …" Kevin pondered.

"Yup."

Kevin was quiet for almost a minute. His furrowed brow indicated he was deep in thought. Bernice gave him silence. At last, Kevin spoke. "Want to do an experiment? See if it's real or not?"

"Uh … what do you mean?"

"You got anywhere to be tonight?" Kevin asked.

"Nope. Was gonna go to a hotel, but they're not expecting me. What's up?"

"Shut your eyes."

Bernice did so. "Why?"

"We're gonna drive around. I'm going to just aimlessly zip around here and there, and at some point I'm going to drive to the swamp. Okay?"

Her stomach churned and she opened her eyes. "No, Kevin—"

"No, wait. Listen. If you keep your eyes shut and I drive you into the swamp but you don't know you're in the swamp, then if the voice stops you know it's real. Right?" An off ramp approached, and Kevin steered them off the expressway.

She blinked at him and thought that through. "Good plan, Kevin." Sorta. Except it was also probably a horrible plan from a safety standpoint. She shouldn't be letting him go back to that place with her. Clearly, he didn't have an accurate understanding of the situation, or he wouldn't be offering to take her back.

"So you wanna do it?"

She bit her lip. "The idea of going back there creeps me out."

"We'll lock the doors and we won't stop for anything. I'll make sure the gas tank is full. It will be fine."

Bernice swallowed heavily, and gave a slow nod. "Okay. Let's do it."

CHAPTER TEN:

THE POWER

AFTER KEVIN FILLED up the tank, Bernice shut her eyes and Kevin began to drive around, making sure to take some dirt roads every now and then since the road to the swamp was a dirt one.

"I really don't think we need to have the music off," Bernice said. Her fists were clenched into tight balls as the voice harassed her. It was definitely getting louder. No question.

"We can switch it back on if you want," Kevin said. "But it'd be interesting to see if the voice gets louder or quieter or whatever when we get within a certain proximity of the swamp. Yeah?"

Bernice sighed, "Commendable scientific thinking there, Kevin."

On they drove.

On and on and on.

At least an hour of driving in silence, except for Bernice periodically updating Kevin on any changes of volume from the voice. She knew she should not be doing this. But a part of her wanted to see what would happen if she heeded the voice. The big problem here was that Kevin was coming, too. She should go alone. It was dangerous, and she should only be endangering herself. Not Kevin. But of course, there was no problem, because of the glaringly obvious fact she kept losing sight of for some idiotic reason: the voice was not the swamp, and the old lady was not a witch or whatever. Swamps did not talk and old ladies did not make vines move.

A helpful thought occurred to Bernice then: of course the vines hadn't really moved; what had happened was the old lady had hit Kevin and Bernice with her hallucination concoction before they'd even realized she'd done so. That's why they'd both witnessed the vines moving. They'd been hallucinating already. Shared hallucinations. Somehow. Yes, that would be it. That was clearly the answer, since in reality vines simply did not move. The supernatural was not real. Swamps did not talk to people in their heads, or in any way at all. Swamps were a conglomeration of water and plants and animals and microbes and elevation and whatnot all coming together to make a certain set of conditions that made the land a swamp. That was what swamps were. Therefore, it naturally followed that Kevin could safely come with her to the swamp.

Come back to the swamp, come back to the swamp.

"I think it's getting quieter," she murmured after a bit.

"Innnteresting ..." he muttered.

She wanted to open her eyes to see why it was so innnteresting, but she refrained. "Kevin, are you sure you're okay with driving into the swamp? What if she like jumps on the windshield and slams her fist through it, or ... uh, lassos the car with a vine? Remember she's super strong."

"We won't be in the swamp long. Just long enough to see if there's a change. Now hush. Listen to the voice. See if it changes anymore."

She leaned her head against the back of the seat and listened. *Come back to the swamp, come back to the swamp.* "I really think it's still getting quieter." She was trying hard not to get too optimistic, but couldn't help thinking that maybe the farther she got the quieter it got. That would be nice. Maybe the power of the swamp lessened with distance? Bah. Power of the swamp? What was she thinking? The swamp had no power. Rebecca had drugs and creepiness on her side, but not magic. Not magic. She tried hard not to think too hard about the moving vine. It was stress. Or a snake. "Definitely quieter."

Kevin uttered a nearly inaudible, "Hmm."

Bernice sat up straighter and tapped his arm excitedly. "Ooh. Kevin. It's super quiet. I can barely hear it."

The car turned and began to bump down a dirt road.

"Wow. Kevin. It's gone," she gasped. "It's gone!"

Kevin muttered something under his breath.

He stopped the car.

"Bernice ..." he started. "Um ..."

Opening her eyes, Bernice looked out at the night. It was dark. Clouds were covering whatever moon there might or might not be. But what she saw shining in the headlights filled her with dread. She directed her gaze at Kevin. "Is this ..."

His hands were on the wheel and he was staring out the windshield with his jaw clenched. "It's the swamp," he said, monotone.

"Oh." She felt a surprising lack of emotions. Numbness. "What does this mean?" she asked Kevin. Why was she asking him? He was no expert on swamp witchcraft. Maybe he would come up with some genius theory she could cling to. Some alternative to her current theory: the swamp was talking to her, and when she left it would drive her crazy telling her to come back over and over until she listened to it and came back and turned into the next Rebecca. "What does this mean?" she repeated when Kevin kept on staring out the window and not answering.

"Um. Well. It's not in your head," he replied. "That's kinda good. Right?"

"Yeah, sorta ..." Bernice mumbled. "Except, if it's not in my head then that means the voice is real. That presents a whole new host of problems, wouldn't you say?"

"Sure." Kevin turned the car on again. "But at least it's nice to know you're not crazy. Yeah? Still, definitely a whole new host of ..." He shifted into drive and hit the gas. The wheels spun. "I think we're stuck in some mud or something."

Bernice felt a sinking feeling in her stomach as a domino effect of reasoning started clicking along in her brain. The voice was real. Therefore, she couldn't deny all the supernatural stuff. Therefore, the old lady wouldn't hurt Bernice since the old lady was the swamp and the swamp wanted Bernice. But, was Kevin in danger? "Don't!" Bernice snapped when Kevin made to open the door to investigate what was preventing the car from moving. "I'll get out and look. You stay put. We are not having a repeat of last year."

"Uh—"

"Just stay."

"Okay, B. Sure," Kevin said hesitantly.

Before opening the door, Bernice scanned what she could of the darkness. She did not see Rebecca. She wished the fact made her feel safe, but it didn't. The old lady was probably just lurking somewhere, camouflaged in the mud and moss. Or she was half the swamp away, but running toward them creepy fast. Bernice gritted her teeth, opened the car door, and stepped out. "Not muddy at all," she said over her shoulder to Kevin. The humid warmth of the swamp enveloped her like a cozy blanket. She shut her eyes a moment, appreciating the comfort of it. It soaked into her skin, energizing her. Despite the stress of the situation, she felt oddly elated. Thrilled, more like.

Kevin said from the car, "Weird. Well, we're definitely stuck on something." He rolled down his window a bit so they could talk while she investigated the car.

She nodded, slammed her door, and walked around the back of the car.

Her jaw dropped. She stared. "No," she muttered as she walked up to the back of the car. "No, no, no." Why had Kevin stopped the car? Why? He had said he wouldn't. The idiot.

Wrapped around the wheels and the bumper and underneath the car, probably entwined around all sorts of car parts, were thick vines of Asiatic bittersweet. She whirled around. "Where are you, Rebecca?" she yelled into the darkness. She didn't even bother attempting to hide the panic in her voice. How was she feeling both panic and elation at the same time? It was disorienting.

"Bernice?" Kevin yelled. "What? Are you okay?" He turned to look at her through the back window.

"Bittersweet's wrapped all around the back of the car. Around the tires and stuff," Bernice called back. She heard his car door opening. "Stay in the car, Kevin!"

He slammed it shut. "Right. But … uh, Bernice, what do we do? You get in here, too."

She ran her hands through her hair and turned in a slow circle, peering into the darkness.

Rebecca stepped out from behind a tree. Or at least Bernice assumed it was Rebecca. A black silhouette with a ratty mess of hair stepped out from behind a tree.

"Get those vines off the car," Bernice growled.

"You returned," Rebecca stated the obvious. "You feel the pull of the swamp. You know that it has chosen you."

"Yes," Bernice growled. "I hear it in my head and it won't shut up. How do I make it stop?"

"You don't. There's no going back. The swamp needs a new ambassador. My time is limited. You are next. It looked inside you and it saw you care for it and—"

"I do not want this," Bernice whispered.

"It wants you. It needs you. You are a part of the swamp now," Rebecca stated, walking closer.

Bernice gritted her teeth and hissed, "But I don't want to be." A part of her knew Rebecca was right. She felt the connection. The elation at being back. But a bigger part of her wanted to fight it and deny it and run away from it as fast as she could.

"Nonsense," Rebecca scoffed. "I know you feel it. The joy. The connectedness."

Bernice didn't answer. Yes, since the moment she had stepped onto the ground in the swamp and felt the air on her skin, she had felt that weird, irrational happiness; the energy humming through her body. But that didn't mean she wanted to be in the swamp. It just meant Rebecca had messed her up with some creepy, evil magic that she'd never asked for.

Rebecca walked closer. "Now that you've returned, I can teach you to use your new abilities. You are the swamp now. Embrace it."

Shaking her head, Bernice backed away. How was Kevin going to get out of this? Would Rebecca hurt him? Was he hearing this conversation?

"There's no running from it. I'll show you—"

73

"Just get those vines off the car."

"No. You need to be here. You need to accept your powers."

"Powers? I don't have powers. Come on. Get the vines off the car."

"You can get the vines off the car."

Bernice blinked. "I can't."

"But you can. And you will. The power is a part of you and you will embrace it."

"I will do no such thing," Bernice growled.

Rebecca sighed and snapped her fingers.

Bernice backed away from Rebecca, looking around wildly. What was going to happen? What had that snap of her fingers done?

Oh.

Bernice glanced down at the vine that had moved from the car to her leg. It was twining around and around, spiraling up from her ankle to her knee, holding her firmly in place. "Let me go."

"You can do it yourself."

"Let me go!" Bernice screamed. "Let me—"

"But you can do it yourself!" Rebecca cut her off eagerly. "Don't you feel it? You can—"

Bernice said, "That's insane! I cannot make a vine move by snapping my fingers, and I will not! Let me go! You have no right—"

Kevin yelled through the open window, "Bernice? What's wrong? What's going on?" He opened the door.

Rebecca's gaze snapped from Bernice to Kevin.

"Don't," Bernice breathed. "Leave him alone." Then she yelled, "Kevin! Stay. In. The. Car!"

"What's she doing to you?" Kevin asked, panicked, half in the car and half out, clearly torn between helping her out and remembering how creepy Rebecca was.

"Don't worry about it!" Bernice answered. "I'll be fine! Shut the door! Lock it!"

Kevin yelled out as, with a jerking motion, he was yanked to the ground. "Bernice!" he screamed as he was pulled beneath the car.

Bernice whirled around to face Rebecca. "Stop it!" she screamed, pulling against the vine wrapped around her leg. She bent to look frantically under the car to try to figure out what was going on. Kevin was struggling, but she couldn't see what was going on. She couldn't get a good look because of the vine holding her. "Please, just let him go! Please!"

Kevin yelled, "Bernice, it's around my neck— I—" *Choke. Gasp.*

Bernice fought to free her leg as she screamed at Rebecca, "Why are you doing this!?"

Rebecca calmly stated, "So that you will test your ability. You won't do it to free yourself, but you will to free him."

"What?" Bernice asked, though she already knew what Rebecca meant; the energy pulsing through her body was practically forcing itself into her mind. "You're insane. I can't—"

"Try," Rebecca said soothingly. "Just try. Feel the plants. Feel their energy. It's easy."

A gasping sound came from beneath the car. Kevin was frantically scrambling in the dirt, his breaths coming short.

"Just shut your eyes and feel them," Rebecca instructed. "You already know how easy it will be to do. Just accept it."

Well, now that Kevin was being strangled by a vine beneath the car, there really was no argument. She could get back to denial just as soon as no one was being murdered. As much as Bernice would have loved to fight the insane, surreal, impossible garbage she felt overtaking her body and her mind, she also knew that the insane, surreal, impossible garbage overtaking her body and her mind was really real and that it would save Kevin. She felt the power humming through her, begging to be used, crowding around the edges of her mind. She gave a weary sigh, shut her eyes, and let the power flow into her. There it was, comfortable and friendly and soothing. She took it and felt with her mind for the vine that was wrapping around Kevin. In a moment, she found it. So easy. There it was—the vine was waiting for her. Just waiting to be told to unwrap itself from Kevin's neck.

So, she told it to unwrap itself.

It listened to her.

Just like that.

"Oh," Bernice said. Well, that had been easy. So, she told the one around her leg to let her go. Then, she kicked at it savagely and flung herself to the ground, reaching under the car. "Kevin!" she gasped. "Are you okay?" She heard him scuffling around, scooting out from underneath the vehicle toward her. He was muttering what sounded like a steady stream of curses under his breath. When he got within reach, she helped him to his feet and put a hand to his neck where the bark of the vine had rubbed his skin raw.

Giving her a wide-eyed, crazy look, he whirled around and sprinted to the driver's side door. He threw it open, got in, and slammed it behind him. She heard the locks click.

Bernice turned back to Rebecca. "I'm leaving."

"All right," Rebecca said calmly.

Bernice began to back away. "What?"

"All right," Rebecca repeated. "Go."

"You're not going to try to stop me?"

"No. You know your power now. You can't deny it anymore. You felt it. You know now that it is good. You will be back. The voice will get stronger and stronger until you have no choice. Go now if you must. You will return."

Bernice shook her head. "You're insane."

"You are the insane one," Rebecca countered. "Why are you fighting the swamp? How can you fight it now that you've felt what it is? It wants you."

"But I don't want it. If I choose the swamp, that means I'm giving up my life."

"But you feel the peace. I know you do. When you sleep, the swamp shows you—" Rebecca stopped short and shut her eyes. She remained motionless for a few seconds, holding up an index finger to indicate to Bernice that she should wait.

"Lady …" Bernice said, watching her in confusion. She backed away a bit more. Why was she not running? "What is up with you?"

Rebecca's eyes snapped open. "If you are indeed as opposed as you seem, the swamp will release you. It does know of a potential alternate host."

"Huh?"

"You are not the only one whose mind I opened to the swamp. Not the only one who breathed the concoction. The swamp saw his mind and—"

"No," Bernice snapped. "No. Stop talking." Rebecca was talking about Kevin. Bernice knew it, and she didn't want to hear it. Back when Rebecca had gotten him with her weird spore concoction, the swamp must have seen into him, too. "No, no, no," she repeated to drown out the sound of Rebecca talking. She backed to the passenger side door and jiggled the handle. Kevin unlocked it. She threw the door open, jumped in, and slammed it shut.

Through Kevin's still open window, Bernice heard Rebecca yell, "The swamp will allow it! You can decide to switch hosts!"

Insane. No. Not an option.

Kevin locked the doors again, as Bernice whirled around to look at Rebecca through the back window.

The old woman was just standing there, smiling a knowing smile.

"Bernice, what do we do? How do we get out of here? Does your phone have reception?"

"Start the car."

"But the vines—"

"Start the car," Bernice cut him off.

He did so.

Bernice shut her eyes. She felt the vines wrapped all around the back of the car. She told them to unwrap themselves. It was cool she didn't have to snap her fingers. That was kinda dorky.

The vines unwrapped themselves.

"The vines are off," she told him. "Go. Go now. Before she makes them go back on." But she knew Rebecca wasn't going to try to make the vines trap them again. The vines were just lying in the dirt road, not moving an inch, finally acting like proper vines instead of some freakish witch minions. Bernice felt them all with her mind. Bernice knew Rebecca wouldn't try anything. Rebecca knew Bernice would make the decision to come back on her own, without any need of convincing.

Well, Rebecca could know it all she wanted. Bernice was never coming back to Cleary Swamp. Never. The voice could scream at her night and day and she'd never go back. She would adapt. She would ignore it. People adapted to all sorts of horrible circumstances and managed to live at least semi-normal lives.

As Kevin tore down the dirt road as fast as he could make the car go, Bernice turned and watched as Rebecca melted into the darkness.

Almost as soon as they'd passed the 'Thank you for visiting Cleary Swamp' sign, the voice started to whisper again in her head.

Come back to the swamp, come back to the swamp.

CHAPTER ELEVEN:

SCRABBLE

Bernice spent her first five days post-swamp in extreme denial. Technically, the first stage of grief. Grief over the perhaps inevitable loss of her life as she knew it, the loss of her dreams, the loss of her identity. Hopefully not the loss of her sanity. But she wasn't just experiencing denial. Was it possible to experience multiple stages all at once?

Denial, sure. Easy. The supernatural was supereasy to deny.

Anger was a given, too. Rebecca had pushed this on her. Bernice was beyond enraged that this had happened to her against her will and that she couldn't stop it.

Bargaining was a bit nebulous. Who was there to bargain with? The swamp? She'd begged and pleaded a bit with Rebecca when she'd had the chance, but it seemed like things were sorta set in stone. The swamp was in her brain and that was all there was to it. Maybe she could switch places with Kevin, but that was awful and selfish and mean, and she was not going to do it.

The fourth step was depression. No problem there. She'd been camped out on Kevin's couch for the past five nights and days, lying around as much as possible, listening to music and watching TV as loud as possible, while the voice got daily (hourly?) louder, and her life got daily (hourly?) more unlivable. Depression was maybe the easiest of all the stages.

Come back to the swamp, come back to the swamp.

Acceptance was the stage she doubted she'd ever reach. Unless she went insane. But then it hardly counted as acceptance, really. Well, she'd find out sooner or later since she was pretty sure she was losing her mind.

At least her power to control plants had disappeared beyond the borders of the swamp. She'd been snapping her fingers at Kevin's philodendron for days with no results.

And the weird elation had gone—the warm, almost loving feeling of comfort that she felt for no good reason when she was in the swamp. Bernice actually found comfort in the depression that had taken its place. The depression made sense given her circumstances. The elation did not. Not at all. She'd take a negative feeling that made sense over a positive one that was creepy and illogical any day.

The evening of her fifth day crashing on Kevin's couch, Bernice was hard at work listening to Queen while concurrently watching one of Kevin's DVDs of the first season of *Space Mantis*. If she was going to go insane, why couldn't she go the kind of insane where she hallucinated *Space Mantis* forever? Now that was a crazy she could get behind if crazy was coming either way. *Come back to the swamp, come back to the swamp.* If only she could pick her insanity at a mental illness buffet line instead of just getting handed her crazy by Rebecca at some sort of hellish restaurant where she couldn't even look at a menu and had to eat whatever the evil waitress brought, maybe at like a gross old roadside diner with deep fried everything. Deep fried roadkill probably. And the evil waitress would force feed it to her. Yes. Bernice's life was fast becoming force fed, deep-fried roadkill. Rancid, probably. Still with bones and fur on under all the deep-fried breading.

Moaning, she flopped back onto the couch.

Kevin walked into the living room. Bernice had not heard the front door open, but that was no surprise since she had the volume of the music and TV up so high. She gave a listless wave at him as he smiled and said a hello she could barely hear. She felt rotten about moping around his living room, blasting music at all hours, eating all his chips, and generally being the worst houseguest ever, but Kevin kept insisting it was fine. He kept saying that if ever a person had a good reason for going off the rails, it was her. He walked over to the couch and flopped down beside her.

Come back to the swamp, come back to the swamp.

Bernice hoped Kevin wasn't too weirded out by her attire. "I hope it's

 80

okay I went through that box marked for donations. The one by the garage door. The thought of going shopping is horrifying." She looked down at what she was wearing—an old T-shirt for some obscure blues band and comfy pajama pants.

"No worries," Kevin said. "You can even help yourself to my actual good clothes. Good thing I'm so scrawny, eh?"

She smiled. "Who'd have thought we wore the same size?"

He smiled a now-familiar conflicted, pitying smile that she was only okay with because at least he was pitying her for the right reasons. He understood what was going on. He asked, "How's things, B? Have a good day?"

"Yep. As long as your TV's volume can exceed the volume of the voice, I count it as a good day."

He frowned. "Bernice, this is—"

"I know," she said, cutting him off before he could specify in what way this situation was pathetic or sad or unsustainable or annoying. She couldn't hear it. She knew it all already. "I know. Kevin, I don't know what to do. I'm so sorry."

"Don't apologize. We'll figure something out, B."

She sighed, trying to fight off tears.

Kevin scooted closer and put an arm around her shoulders, pulling her into a hug. "We'll figure something out."

She nodded against his shoulder, though she didn't believe for a second that they'd be able to figure something out, and she knew he didn't believe it for a second either.

Kevin cleared his throat. "Uh, B?"

"Yeah?"

He sighed. "I gotta tell you something. It's about a … uh, solution. I think. Maybe."

Bernice gave him a questioning look. "What?" Whatever he was going to say, it was clear it wasn't good.

"Okay. So here's the thing, B. You know when we were in the swamp and that vine was strangling me—"

"Yep," Bernice replied, "I do recall that."

"Um, so. Well. I kinda heard a voice. In my head."

Bernice gasped. No. So the swamp really had gotten into him. No.

"I haven't heard it again since, so I figured maybe it was just the … ya know, like the strangling doing weird stuff to my brain. Lack of air and all that. But, see, the voice kinda said it wanted me. If you rejected it, it said it'd take me instead."

Bernice blinked. She shook her head. "No." All that stuff Rebecca had said after Kevin had been attacked by the vine came back to her. The stuff about Kevin being an alternate host if Bernice really was so dead set against the swamp. The swamp had told Kevin the same thing it had told Rebecca.

"You know anything about that?" Kevin asked.

"No. No, I do not. And that's insane. I think you're right. It was just lack of air to your brain."

"But—"

"Kevin, no. Don't be an idiot. You were in the swamp when you heard the voice in your head, right?"

"Yep."

"Well, see, that's proof it wasn't the swamp. I only hear the voice when I'm *not* in the swamp."

"Um. Doesn't Rebecca hear the voice when she's in the swamp? It must communicate with her—"

"Just stop it. You're not going to—"

"Bernice, my life is already destroyed. The murder thing, dropping out of school, quitting my music. Everything's a mess."

"You can fix it. Just because things are messy for you now doesn't mean you need to go turn into some mad, mud-coated swamp lunatic. You can fix your life up just fine, Kevin."

"But you can fix yours, too—"

"Shut up. I've destroyed your life enough, Kevin. I'm not destroying it more."

"Bernice," he said, "you have not destroyed—"

"Yes I have. It started the moment I took you to the swamp that first time, and it's gotten worse and worse ever since."

"Bernice—"

She turned to him and stared him down. "Kevin. We will not talk about this anymore. Listen. Fine. You're right. You are right that the swamp has decided you could be an alternate host. Yes. Rebecca told me that night. I know it. But here's the thing, Kevin. She also told me it was my decision to make. And I'm never going to make that decision. So you can just shut up about it." She leaned back against his arm, shaking.

He cleared his throat, and opened his mouth to speak.

"Shut up."

He nodded.

They sat in awkward silence for a bit listening to Freddy Mercury. She wished she was a champion, but it was more likely that she was going to bite the dust. Much more likely.

After a bit, Kevin said over the music, "A storm's gonna be rolling in tonight. I'm going to just go make sure all the windows are shut. When I'm back, wanna play a game?" Every night, they'd been playing board games late into the night until Bernice was too tired to keep her eyes open. It was great distraction from the voice. At least in her dreams there was no voice. But her dreams were all of the swamp. Super soothing, beautiful, vivid dreams of nature. Birds singing, gentle breezes blowing, baby ducks paddling along in the water behind their mother.

She hated the dreams more than she had ever hated her worst nightmare. She knew the dreams were just the swamp trying to convince her to return.

"Sure," she mumbled. "Scrabble?" Kevin was almost as good at Scrabble as she was. The challenge was nice. If she went to the swamp (which she wasn't going to do) there would certainly be no more Scrabble. Rebecca probably wouldn't want to scratch word games in the mud, and the swamp most certainly wouldn't. Even though it probably could if it wanted to.

"Sure. Scrabble it is." He gave her shoulders a reassuring sort of squeeze, then got up to check the windows.

She felt sick. Kevin was so nice. If this insanity got him in trouble again she'd never forgive herself. She hated that he now knew he was an alternate host. She could just see him trying to be a hero and going to the swamp behind her back to offer himself up. "Oh!" Bernice said to his back. "How did your meeting go?" Kevin had, at Bernice's near-begging insistence, set up a meeting with Professor Zimmer about getting back into the program.

Kevin stopped and turned. "It went good! Looks like I'm probably gonna be back in next semester if I get the right paperwork done and get some references." He paused and added, "Uh, she wanted me to tell you hi from her."

"Oh, yeah. Tell her hi from me next time you see her." Bernice didn't really want to think about Professor Zimmer and the school and the direction her life could have taken if all this hadn't happened. "Anyway. That's awesome. Congratulations, Kevin."

He grinned. "Yeah, thanks for pushing me to go on and talk to her." He turned and walked off.

Come back to the swamp, come back to the swamp.

Bernice gritted her teeth. This had to stop. She could not adapt. It was getting harder, not easier. Louder and louder and louder. The thing that she hated most of all (At least, maybe most of all. It was so hard to pick what she hated most about her situation) was that she found herself looking forward to sleep—leaving her real life behind with all its confusion and stress and fear and the stupid, stupid voice, and surrendering to sleep and the peaceful swamp dreams. This was, of course, the swamp's plan. She could feel it convincing her to return. She could feel the swamp implying that only in the swamp would she have the peace she so desperately needed. She was starting to dread her waking life intensely. It was a horrible feeling.

Bernice woke with a start. A huge crash of thunder had woken her. Her dream had been entrancing—insects had been humming drowsily in the background, and she'd been lying in the moss watching a spider spin a web in an alder above her head. The sun had been warm, the breeze had been soothing, everything had been beautiful. But, of course, the moment Bernice woke the voice started up again. *Come back to the swamp, come back to the swamp.*

And there was no background noise to block it out.

Where was the background noise?

She felt a stab of rage. Had Kevin turned off the TV before he'd gone to bed?

She threw off the blanket Kevin must have put over her after the Scrabble games had knocked her out, then she sat and fumbled around in the dark for the remote control. It was usually on the coffee table. Where was it? Why was it so dark? She looked at the screen of her phone, which was also on the coffee table. A bit past 9 a.m.

Over the sound of rain on the windowpanes and the voice in her head, Bernice heard Kevin trotting down the stairs. Weird. He was usually at work by 8. She turned toward the hallway. Lightning flashed as Kevin walked into the room. "Hey, B. Power's out," he announced. In a second flash of lightning, she caught his anxious expression. He knew what this meant in regard to the voice.

"Why aren't you at work?" she asked as she searched frantically for the remote control.

"Not going in today."

"Why?"

"Don't worry about it."

"Is it because of me?" she asked, feeling guilt wash over her. Was he skipping work to look after her? Again?

"Remote's lost?" Kevin asked, not answering her question.

"Yes. Help me look."

He began to search. "You tried my headphones with your phone?"

"They don't go loud enough anymore," she said, cringing at how positively unhinged her voice sounded, all shrill and panicked.

"Um, even if we find the remote, the power is, uh, out …" he pointed out.

She halted in her frenzied search. "Oh. Yeah."

"Wanna go for a drive? We can turn up the radio."

She was on her feet in an instant, heading toward the garage. Kevin followed.

Bernice put her hands to her temples and scrunched her eyes shut. She stumbled as she walked through the kitchen, and ran into the kitchen table, reeling from the impact.

"Bernice, you okay?" Kevin questioned, grabbing her by the elbow and helping her stumble along toward the garage.

She shook her head, and a whimper escaped her lips. "Kevin … I can't do this anymore."

"Come on," he said, his voice thick with worry. "Come on, B. Let's just get you in the car and turn up the music. The music and the rain on the car and all that … it'll help."

Temporarily, maybe. Maybe. But even if it could be drowned out, it wouldn't be able to be for much longer. Two or three days, tops, at the rate at which the volume had been increasing.

Bernice kept her eyes squeezed shut, and let Kevin guide her to the car. He opened the door and helped her in, then got into the driver's seat, turned on the car, cranked up the radio, and set out. She wasn't sure how long they drove. She was vaguely aware that rain was pounding the roof of the car so hard that it felt dangerous to be driving. "Is this safe?" she asked Kevin.

"Sure. I'm going slow. No one's on the road."

She slipped into a daze. Not sleep, though. Sleep would have been nice. Peaceful. This was just a haze of *come back to the swamp, come back to the swamp* and horrible 90's pop, punctuated with weight loss commercials and pathetic DJ banter. After who knows how long, she heard herself say, "Kevin. Drive me to the swamp."

"No way, Bernice. No."

"I can't take this anymore."

"Bernice, you don't mean—"

"Drive me to the swamp!" She squeezed her hands into tight fists, her nails digging into her skin. Why wouldn't the voice stop? Why? She didn't want this. Couldn't it see how much she did not want this? *Come back to the swamp, come back to the swamp.*

"Bernice—"

"Now!"

Kevin gripped the wheel tight and yelled back frantically, "Bernice, we can figure this out! There are other ways—"

"You are *not* switching places with me, Kevin! No!"

"Not that!" he yelled. "Yesterday I got together a list of mediums and stuff … ya know, like those people who say they do magic stuff. I was gonna call them tomorrow. Most must be fake but maybe someone's real. Yeah? Bernice," he said, taking a calming breath and reaching over to put a hand over one of her tightly clenched fists, "we'll figure this out. We will."

She began to sob, but she nodded. She could manage one more day. Or maybe he could bring her to the swamp right now and just bring the mediums out there … yes, that might work … but no. Someone would find out that Kevin had again been the last person to see her before she disappeared. Some camera somewhere would catch him driving her to the swamp, and driving from the swamp alone. She would not cause Kevin to be suspected of her murder again. Twice would be a coincidence so huge that no amount of rich whiteness could save him. He'd go to prison for sure. For a long, long time.

So, no, he could not bring her to the swamp tonight. Because she knew—somehow, she was certain—that the next time she went back to the swamp she wouldn't be able to leave again. Wouldn't be able to, or wouldn't want to, or whatever. Maybe by then it would be the same thing. When she went back—if? Please, if, not when—she wouldn't be leaving again.

If she went back, it would be because she had decided to become the swamp.

CHAPTER TWELVE:

NO WITNESSES

AT SOME POINT, Bernice fell asleep in the car. As always, she dreamt of the swamp. It was night. The stars were bright, it was gently raining, some bird she couldn't identify by call was singing.

When Bernice woke, the voice instantly filled her skull, yelling, over and over and over. Louder than ever. The car radio didn't come close to drowning it out.

COME BACK TO THE SWAMP, COME BACK TO THE SWAMP.

Bernice exhaled a breath and felt cold resignation wash over her at the sound. For a few moments, she just listened to it. Soaked up the sound of it. Noticed for the first time that though it was most certainly a voice saying words, she couldn't tell what the voice actually sounded like. She was sensing the words. Not hearing the words. It was loud like a voice, but there was no actual voice. On the one hand, very weird. But on the other hand, perhaps it made perfect sense. After all, it was not an actual sound from her surroundings creating sound waves and entering her ear. It was in her head.

Bernice opened her eyes. She was curled up on the passenger seat of Kevin's car. Kevin was asleep in the driver's seat, his head resting against the steering wheel. He looked uncomfortable. His neck was going to hurt like crazy when he woke. His neck that still had red scratches from the vine that had nearly strangled him. Poor Kevin.

COME BACK TO THE SWAMP, COME BACK TO THE SWAMP.

Bernice looked out the windows. Kevin had driven them down a dirt road in the middle of a forest. He must have known it from some research project he'd been a part of back when he'd been a student. He must have picked somewhere secluded so that they could keep the radio going and not end up with the cops being called.

She pulled out her phone. She had reception. Great. She had to do a few things before Kevin woke up.

His idea about the mediums was going to fail. There was no such thing as real mediums. She was aware that doubting mediums when she heard a swamp talking in her head and could control plants' movements with her mind was some kind of hypocrisy or narrow-mindedness or something. But still, she knew the medium idea was Kevin grasping at straws. She knew it would fail. In the unlikely event that there was anyone in the entire world who could help her out, there was no way she could track the person down in time to get help before she lost her mind. And, therefore, she had to get a few things in order before she did what she had to do. She had to act before she went crazy for real, and she had to act before Kevin decided to try to be a hero, which couldn't be too far off considering what a White Knight type the poor guy was.

First, she sent an email to Professor Zimmer, telling her thanks for allowing Kevin back in the program and letting the professor know that Bernice would be more than happy to be a reference for Kevin if he needed one; but that she'd have to get back to Bernice by that evening if a reference was required.

Then, Bernice tracked down the club Kevin's band used to play at. They had open mic timeslots every night. Bernice found their number. So as not to wake Kevin, she quietly snuck out of the car to make the call. They had a few open time slots. She signed him up for one. Now, it would just be a matter of getting him to go. It would take a lot of convincing, especially since he knew the state she was in. Well, she'd just have to exert as much effort as she could at pretending that she was doing better. It would be quite an undertaking considering that the voice was screaming in her skull, but it was just one day.

Just one day.

She could do it.

He needed to think she was improving. That way, he wouldn't suspect. And, that way, he wouldn't be thinking in terms of going to the swamp to trade places with her.

Bernice was parked on Kevin's couch again watching season three of *Space Mantis* when she got an email back from Professor Zimmer. She read the email through with confusion. Professor Zimmer had no idea what Bernice was talking about. The professor had not met with Kevin. As much as she would have been interested in talking with Kevin about coming back, he had not met with her.

Kevin had lied to Bernice.

Bernice braced against the voice and listened to Kevin moving around in the kitchen, making lunch. Why had he lied? He'd probably not wanted to admit he'd spent the day running down leads on a bunch of frauds who said they had magical abilities in order to make a quick buck off the gullible. Stupid Kevin. And there she'd been thinking he was getting his life back on track. Well, after today he'd be able to. There'd be nothing standing in his way. Or, not standing per se, but lying on his couch.

He walked into the living room, a happy grin on his face and a tray of food in his hands.

She swallowed her anger. He'd been so happy ever since she'd told him the lie about how she was starting to become accustomed to the voice. The lie where she'd said it had stopped getting louder.

COME BACK TO THE SWAMP, COME BACK TO THE SWAMP.

"Grilled cheese and tomato soup," he said, setting the tray down on the coffee table with a flourish.

"Thanks, Kevin." She gave him a smile she hoped looked genuine. Pretending not to be plagued by the screaming voice was a huge strain. Leaning forward, she grabbed a sandwich.

He took a mug of soup and sat down beside her and nodded toward the TV. "Which one's this?"

"Captain Joe's chasing after the rogue Central officer who kidnapped his sister," she filled him in.

"Ah. This is a good one," Kevin said, settling in and sipping his soup.

"They're all good ones."

"Truth." Sip.

COME BACK TO THE SWAMP, COME BACK TO THE SWAMP.

"Why aren't you at work?" Bernice asked.

"Day off, B," he said as he rested his feet on the coffee table.

Bernice doubted it, but didn't pursue the issue. "Do me a favor."

"Sure. What?" he asked, then took another sip.

"I got you a gig at that club down by campus. The one you and your band used to play. Open mic tonight at 9. Do it."

COME BACK TO THE SWAMP, COME BACK TO THE SWAMP.

He turned to stare at her. "Bernice—" he started.

"Kevin. Please. I need to see you getting back into the stuff you used to do before all this swamp stuff."

"Bernice, that's really nice of you and all, but I just don't know if I can."

"I need you to. Kevin. Please." She heard the quaver in her voice.

He heard it, too, and studied her face in silence for a few moments. "Why? What's up?"

She sighed. "I just feel so bad. You know, I used to think you were so annoying. All laid back and cool, with your guitar and your artsy loner thing and all that. But now all that stuff's gone and you're so regular, it just makes me really sad because it's because of me."

"Bernice, don't think like that."

She took a bite of sandwich and looked away from him. Tears sprung to her eyes. She welcomed their good timing even though they felt a tad manipulative.

"Hey now," he murmured, concerned, putting an arm around her shoulders. "Bernice, if it really means that much to you then I'll do it."

She swallowed a lump in her throat, and said, "Thanks, Kevin."

"We still gotta call those mediums though and see if any of them can help you out."

"That can wait," she said. "Do it tomorrow or something. I really think I'm adapting."

"Okay, if you're sure. That's pretty cool, B. I knew you could do it."

"Yep."

COME BACK TO THE SWAMP, COME BACK TO THE SWAMP.

They directed their attention to *Space Mantis* for a bit even though neither of them were really watching. Kevin kept casting he sidelong glances that she kept ignoring while trying to appear normal and calm. It was worse than running a marathon.

After a while, Kevin said, "I haven't played in a long time, but I can do some slow stuff or something."

"Whatever you play will be fine."

"I should probably practice." He reclaimed his arm and stood up.

She nodded and watched him walk off. The second he was out of the room, she scrunched her eyes shut and succumbed to the agony of the screaming voice.

Just a few more hours.

At last, evening came. 8:00. One hour until Kevin's time slot at the club. He'd been up in his room practicing for hours. Bernice had stayed downstairs, ostensibly finishing up the DVD of *Space Mantis*, but really just suffering through the voice yelling at her over and over and over as time ticked by agonizingly slowly.

She was lying on the couch with a blanket over her head when she heard through the yelling, "Hey, B."

She composed her features into some expression that hopefully didn't seem tortured, and pushed the blanket down. Kevin was standing behind the couch, looking down at her. "Hiya," she said, noticing that he hadn't shaved. It made her happy to see him looking a bit more like scruffy old laid back Kevin. And he was wearing the old blues band T-shirt. The one she'd found in the donation box. Even better. If he was wearing ratty old jeans, then her day was made. She sat up and looked at his legs. Ratty jeans. Score.

"Hey, Bernice," he said with a smile. "I'm gonna head over. You're coming to watch, right?"

"Of course I am," she lied. She didn't want to be anywhere near Kevin tonight. No security cameras were going to catch them even remotely in the same vicinity that evening. "I'm just gonna try to scrounge up a more club-appropriate outfit. Maybe go track down Kate and see if she's got anything I can borrow."

"Cool," he said. "She called me yesterday asking about you. She'd like to see you."

"Cool. So I'll just get some clothes from her and then I'll head on over in time for your time slot."

COME BACK TO THE SWAMP, COME BACK TO THE SWAMP.

"I'll drive you."

Shoot. Well, she could pretend to walk up to Kate's door and then dodge away when Kevin drove off. "Thanks," she said, standing up and heading toward the garage.

"Don't you need your purse?" Kevin asked from behind her. "Or your phone?"

She'd left them both on the coffee table. The money in her pocket was all she needed. "Oh. Yeah. Of course."

He grabbed them and gave them to her, then they headed out to the car.

Once he'd buckled his guitar into the back seat, they were set to go.

"It's awesome you're doing so much better. Like yesterday you is a completely different person from today you," he said as they drove down the driveway and toward campus. "So it's just that you're … like, adapting to the voice?"

"Yep." It was good to hear she was fooling him. The strain of pretending to be fine was near unbearable, but if it was working then that gave her the strength to keep it up a bit longer. "It's weird. I woke up this morning and I just sorta decided to embrace it. Just let it be a part of me. Quit fighting it. Quit being mad at it. And it's still there, but it's not the same. Like it can be there and be a part of me but not destroy me." Nice. That sounded good. If only it were true.

"Wow. Cool. Very … spiritual … or something. Way to go, B."

"Thanks."

COME BACK TO THE SWAMP, COME BACK TO THE SWAMP.

They listened to the radio in silence. Bernice would have liked to talk. She would have liked to thank him for everything. There was so, so much she'd have liked to say to him. But if she got all sentimental and effusive, it would tip him off that something was up. So she just listened to the music. The most she allowed herself to do was reach over and take his hand that wasn't on the wheel.

He squeezed her fingers, shot her a smile, and looked back at the road.

They drove into the apartment complex Kate lived at, and Kevin pulled up in front of the right building. "Remember, apartment 5," he said.

"Gotcha." Bernice released his hand, opened the door, and got out.

"Hey, Bernice," he laughed. "You forgot your purse again."

She winced, then turned. "Oh, thanks!" How was she going to dispose of it where it wouldn't be found and considered evidence? His fingerprints were one it. Not cool. Well, she could just bring it with her. The swamp would probably take care of it somehow. If it could hide a person, it could hide a purse.

He handed it to her. "See ya soon!"

"See ya soon." Not. "If I don't see you before you go on, break a leg," she said. Aw shoot. She felt tears threatening to spring into her eyes. She needed to get away fast.

"Will do, B," he replied with a happy grin that hurt her heart.

She turned and walked to the front door of Kate's building.

Kevin drove off. Once he had turned around the corner at the end of the road, Bernice moved away from the building and walked across the lawn heading toward the campus's main street, where she could catch a taxi. She'd have to wait until 9 o'clock to actually get the taxi—Kevin's performance time; the time when a club full of witnesses would be able to give him an alibi for the time she went missing.

So, until 9 o'clock, she'd kill time wandering around town, making sure to stand conspicuously in front of a few security cameras and have a few memorable conversations with storekeepers.

COME BACK TO THE SWAMP, COME BACK TO THE SWAMP.

"I'm coming, I'm coming," she muttered. "Hold on."

EPILOGUE

"PROFESSOR JAMES!" YELLED one of the undergrads from across the clearing.

Kevin looked in her direction. What the heck was that kid's name? Emily? Elizabeth? One of those. Some variation of Elizabeth, he was pretty sure. One thing he'd noticed over the decades at the university: name fads came and name fads went, but there was at least one kid with a variation of Elizabeth every year. Almost three decades on the job, and Elizabeth/Beth/Liz/Eliza remained a constant.

"Yeah?" he called back across the swamp at her, leaving off her name. He wasn't so sure she was an Elizabeth after all. "What's up?" Kevin was preoccupied. He was always preoccupied when his work brought him out to Cleary Swamp. The voice had a tendency to whisper at the back of his brain whenever he was there, and he did not like the voice.

He didn't come out too often, but this swamp had a great sampling of native swamp flowers that was perfect for his botany lab.

"I think I found a rose mallow," maybe-Elizabeth hollered.

He winced at her holler and began to slog through the mud over to her. Why was she being so loud? He reached her and looked where she was pointing. "Hey, good job. That is, indeed, a rose mallow." He summoned the lab over, said some relevant stuff about the flower in question, and sent them on their way to hunt for more plants. Kevin remained by the flower, crouching down and inspecting the petals. He smiled. Swamp rose mallow had been one of Bernice's favorites. Was one of her favorites. And Cleary Swamp had an unexplainable disproportionate amount of swamp rose mallow. Cleary Swamp had an unexplainable disproportionate amount of all sorts of native plants, actually. And an equally disproportionate lack of invasive species.

It was a mystery to the scientists who did their research there. After Professor Zimmer had retired a few years back, Kevin had kept up her yearly inventory of the swamp's plant life. He pretended to scratch his head along with the scientific community about why there were nearly no invasive species in the swamp, but he knew the reason. It was Bernice. The changes hadn't started occurring until the year she disappeared. After that, year after year the native plant diversity had grown more and more impressive, while the invasives had dwindled to the point where they were a downright rarity. There were no signs that plants had been cut, or sprayed, or anything. They just simply got less and less plentiful, as though some force was convincing them year after year to disperse their seeds outside the borders of the swamp, and scoot their root structures inch by inch toward the swamp's perimeter. Almost as though—Kevin thought with a smile—there was some invasive species specialist turned swamp witch with the power to influence the movement of plants.

There was no way in hell Kevin would ever begin to even hint about the possibility of a supernatural explanation, so he just kept on studying the 'mystery' year after year, since it was a nice chance to reminisce about the weird old days with Bernice. The more time passed, the more he could think of that episode of his life as an adventure instead of a nightmare.

If only it hadn't ended with Bernice disappearing again.

Kevin didn't mind that he had the answer to the mystery of that swamp and no one else ever would. It amused him to hear the theories getting more and more crazy as time went by. And crazy the theories were. How could a rational mind explain that wind and animals weren't dispersing invasive seeds into the swamp like they dispersed them everywhere else? And if the seeds were being dispersed in the swamp, there was no way a rational mind could explain why the seeds weren't germinating. Not just one species not germinating. But all the invasive species. And just the invasives. Not the natives.

One of his personal favorite crazy theories was that Cleary Swamp was a secret test site for a new selective herbicide that targeted only invasive species. Idiotic. Such an herbicide simply could not exist, and it made him cringe a bit to even hear them toss around the possibility. That level of selectivity was just impossible in an herbicide. And even if it had been possible, no one with such an amount of money to fund something that out there would deem invasives a cause worthy of dumping all that money into. Also, things were never perfect on the first try, and thus during tests the wrong plants would be killed until the kinks were worked out, to say nothing of unforeseen consequences for the surrounding environment; poisoned water, birth defects in local populations, etc. That sort of testing was the sort of testing that was not done on American soil. That sort of testing was done in poor, developing countries where it was easier to get away with being an unethical monster.

Another of Kevin's favorite of his colleagues' theories was that environmental crusaders came to the swamp under cover of darkness, eradicating every last invasive, then snuck out before dawn, not leaving a trace. But, of course, even if a big group of people cared enough about invasives to go to all the trouble of being nefarious like that, there would still be no point. There was no conceivable reason they wouldn't come during daylight to do the same thing, just with better lighting and with the possibility of volunteer credits or experience for a resume.

Nope, all their rational minds could not figure it out. He could never, ever admit to believing in a supernatural explanation. Professors of botany did not generally believe in magic. But then, professors of botany did not generally have a personal experience with being strangled by a vine from a talking swamp.

He sometimes found himself getting a bit of a supercilious attitude about it, until he stopped and realized that if there was one phenomenon that had an honest-to-goodness supernatural explanation, then it logically followed that other unexplainable phenomena might be explained by the supernatural as well. After all, the odds of him being in the know about the only bit of supernatural in the world were quite slim. This opened up a whole can of worms; the placebo effect, Naga fireballs, the building of

Stonehenge, ghosts, psychics. Hell, Sasquatch was probably real. How often had he dreamt up idiotic explanations for the unexplainable like his colleagues were doing for the lack of invasives at Clearly Swamp?

Kevin shook his head and watched the undergrads walking around, hopefully not stepping on anything rare. But even if they did trample something important, Bernice would see to it that it was replaced.

After a bit, Kevin gathered them all together and they talked about their findings. "Okay," he said at last. "Crash course in compass use. Find your own way back to the van. I'll be a few minutes behind you."

"You mean we gotta navigate alone?" one boy asked. The kid was a freshman. The only freshman in the class.

Everyone rolled their eyes at him.

"Yep," Kevin answered.

The freshman continued, "But … Professor James, this place is totally haunted or something. By that one girl—"

A girl beside him gave him a sharp elbow to the ribs.

"Oh. Yeah …" the freshman muttered.

The students all got awkward. Rumors of Kevin's murder accusation sure had stuck over the years.

Kevin sighed. "Look, the swamp's not haunted, and I'm not a murderer. Go ahead and check. It's public record. Tons of evidence. You all head on back to the van."

Pulling out their compasses, they turned and headed off, some of them shooting apologetic glances back at Kevin, while others began to mock the freshman for believing in ghosts.

Kevin watched them walk off, then headed north toward Bernice's old research plot. The willow was still there, nearly dead. He moseyed up to it and pulled out his pocket knife. There, right at eye level, was the B he'd carved into the bark the year she'd disappeared the second time. Sure, as a botany professor, he should not be carving into a tree trunk. But when one was friends with a swamp witch who one hadn't seen in three decades, one had to communicate how one could. He ran his fingers over the B he'd carved, then over the K that had appeared beside the B a few years later. Under the B he had scratched in a tally mark for every time he'd returned. Sixty-two tally marks so far. Under the K, there were twenty-one.

No—twenty-two.

There was a new one.

Bernice had been back to the tree sometime between last fall and this summer.

Kevin was about to go meet up with the students when suddenly the voice filled his head.

She needs help.

Kevin froze. He shook his head.

She needs help.

He swallowed heavily and looked around. What? While it was not at all uncommon for him to hear the voice in his head when he was in Cleary Swamp, it was always quiet and muddled and incoherent. Not loud and clear like this, filling his skull.

She needs help.

Kevin put a hand to the trunk to steady himself as a wave of dizziness washed over him. He blinked and stared at the tally marks. "What, Bernice?" he muttered. Then he noticed something else scratched into the willow bark, around the tree to the right of the tally marks. He walked around to check it out.

Scratched in the trunk was a message of sorts: ? – R – B – ?

Kevin squinted at the message and ran his hand across it. Well … Okay. R was Rebecca and B was Bernice. The first question mark had to be for Rebecca's predecessor. So the second one was Bernice's successor. The second question mark was underlined, and she'd left this thing as a message for him. Why?

Kevin swallowed. His heart rate picked up.

The swamp wanted him to find a successor for Bernice.

Bernice was going to do to someone else what Rebecca had done to her. And the swamp wanted his help. Needed his help, if the swamp voice was to be believed, which he supposed it must be. Could swamps lie?

Was Bernice sick? Why was a replacement needed? She was only fifty-five. Maybe the swamp needed his help because Bernice was refusing to find a replacement herself?

He took a few steps away from the tree, still staring at the message.

"Professor James?" came a voice from behind him.

Kevin turned to find one of his students, Jason, standing a few paces away, eyeing him questioningly. The kid was wearing a vintage *Space Mantis* tee shirt—the show was experiencing a resurgence in popularity. Kevin couldn't help but smile at the sight of the shirt, since it made him think of pre-swamp Bernice.

Kevin turned away from the half-dead willow and said to Jason, "Did you get lost on the way to the van?" He doubted it. Jason was easily one of the program's best students. He could identify every flower, every tree, every bird. He set the curve in every class from wetlands to policy to statistics. And not only did the kid have the technical stuff down, he loved it. He loved it all. Jason wouldn't get lost in the swamp. The kid wasn't capable of being lost in nature. He was probably born with a flawless internal compass in his brain.

Jason had a great future ahead of him.

Maybe …

But, on the other hand, something had just occurred to Kevin …

"Nope, Professor. Not lost. I just got distracted." He waved his phone at Kevin. "I was taking pictures of some flowers. I found some super cool stuff." He walked to Kevin's side, shoved his phone in Kevin's face, and began to scroll through some images.

"Oh, wow," Kevin exclaimed, impressed. "Could you send me those?"

"Sure thing."

They began to walk back to the van.

Jason said, "This swamp is crazy beautiful. So cool."

"Mmm," said Kevin. "Hey, what's that you're carrying?" He'd just spotted some hedge clippers in Jason's hand.

"Oh, I tripped over these when I was back over there." Jason waved the clippers in the direction of a clump of alders. "They were stuck in a tussock of grass. Figured I'd bring them back to campus and dispose of them properly."

Kevin held out his hand for the clippers, his heart hammering. Had he just seen …

Jason handed the clippers over.

Kevin stared at them. Yes. Most of the stickers were peeled off or faded beyond recognition, but there was one that showed Aragorn waving Anduril over his head heroically. Super quality adhesive and sealant on that sticker to have lasted three decades in a swamp.

Jason had found Bernice's old hedge clippers.

Kevin cleared his throat. He sighed. Then he spoke. "Hey, Jason, do you have a summer job lined up yet?"

"Nope, Professor," Jason answered, scanning through his photos as he walked over roots and tussocks of grass, not tripping once. "Why?"

"I've got an opening if you're interested in cataloging the plant species in the swamp this summer."

ACKNOWLEDGEMENTS

Thanks and love to my family: Will, Anna, Julia, Pat, Steve, Katie, Niko, Nick, Ben, Stephanie, Mike, Stella, Holly, and Bill.

Thanks to Melissa Ringsted for her editing expertise and for making me look like a pro at the technical aspects of writing, to Najla Qamber for the beautiful cover art, to Rebecca Poole for the lovely interior layout, and, of course, to Lindy Ryan for reading Swamp and thinking that it would be a good fit for Black Spot Books. I'm thrilled beyond belief that Come Back to the Swamp found such a great home.

Thanks to Jennifer Flath for being a thorough and thoughtful first reader. Thanks to the Fish Climbing Trees for being such great and supportive writer friends. Thanks to my pals at Spaceboy Books. To Margaret Atwood, Kurt Vonnegut, and PG Wodehouse for inspiring me with their amazing writing.

And thanks to all the people I haven't mentioned but who have helped to make me the writer I am by your support or just by teaching me something about human nature. Friends, extended family, every writer I've ever read, and random strangers on the street whose quirkiness or awesomeness stuck with me.

ABOUT THE AUTHOR

Laura Morrison lives in the Metro Detroit area with her husband, daughters, cats, and vegetable garden. She has a B.S. in applied ecology and environmental science from Michigan Technological University. Before she was a writer and stay-at-home mom, she battled invasive species and researched turtles. Her novel, Grimbargo, is published with Spaceboy Books.

CPSIA information can be obtained
at www.ICGtesting.com
Printed in the USA
LVHW04s1502120918
589921LV00011B/1017/P